The Hero of Vane City

Bribery, theft and even murder were the weapons used by Mayor Tobias Vane and his cousin – Marshal Nathan Harlow – to control Vane City. But all that looked set to change when the Bullen gang hit town, thirsting for revenge and well aware the marshal was a cowardly fraud.

What the gang didn't know, however, was that Will Vane, the mayor's nephew, was not only an honest man but a brilliant shootist determined to uphold the law whatever the cost.

Soon, bullets began to fly and both the jail and Boot Hill had new customers! One day, if Will could survive knife and bullet, Vane City would at last experience the justice it had never known.

The Hero of Vane City

TOM BENSON

A Black Horse Western

ROBERT HALE · LONDON

© Tom Benson 2001
First published in Great Britain 2001

ISBN 0 7090 7032 2

Robert Hale Limited
Clerkenwell House
Clerkenwell Green
London EC1R 0HT

Typeset by
Derek Doyle & Associates, Liverpool.
Printed and bound in Great Britain by
Antony Rowe Limited, Wiltshire.

ONE

Nathan Harlow sat back in the old chair. It was tilted dangerously on two legs so that his feet could rest on the hitching rail in front of the marshal's office. The day was hot, with the blazing sun not far short of high noon, and the lawman was tired and just about ready to doze off. His large belly heaved contentedly and his unshaven face with its full red lips and large, bulbous nose, shone greasily.

He liked Vane City. He had been born there, not long after his Uncle Ned had founded it during the gold-rush period. It had been a busy and prosperous place then and to call it a city might have been the right thing to do at the time. But those days were over. The ore had been worked out; cattle prices were low, and only the lumber business, a little quarrying, and a new influx of small homesteaders kept the shabby place on the map.

And that was why he liked it. Nathan Harlow

5

was not a marshal who wanted trouble. The quiet life suited him. He was a popular local figure. A nephew of the founder, cousin of the mayor, and widower of Jessie Penrose, whose father had preached the gospel with a gun in one hand and a Bible in the other. Nathan was a link with the great days. He was part of the history of Vane City.

As he dozed in the heat, so did the rest of the town. The stores closed for a midday meal, and the school let out with a sudden noise that quickly died away as the children left the street to be fed.

It was the clatter of a horse that woke Nathan from his doze. It came from the north end of the main street and he opened one eye to see who was fool enough to ride out when all sensible folk were at home eating or sleeping.

It was a stranger on a scraggy cow pony. He was a rough-looking character, thin and unshaven, with dark, dusty clothes and a serviceable Colt at his side. There was an old Winchester in a saddle holster and a trail coat that was folded behind him. The marshal watched as the man passed the jail-house without as much as a sign that he saw the lawman sitting there. He rode on down the street until reaching the Golden Horse saloon and dismounted there, tethering his mount to the hitching rail. He looked around in a casual manner and then entered the building.

He was out again a moment or two later. There

had been no time to take a drink, and the marshal stirred uneasily as the man mounted again and rode off down the dusty street to turn right near Kendrews' grain store and disappear among the small houses that spread out towards the river.

Nathan Harlow felt slightly disturbed by what had happened. He had a feeling that the man was somebody he should know, and he also wondered why he had gone to the saloon instead of coming to the marshal for whatever information he needed. It was obvious that he had made some enquiry before continuing his journey. Nathan moved his feet from the rail, hitched up his gunbelt, and strode purposefully across the street to the Golden Horse. His boots stirred up a fine dust among the dry, crumbling ruts.

The saloon was a drab building with the gilding dull around the tarnished mirrors, the walls in need of paint, and a fine film of dust over everything. There were only two customers, both elderly and talking quietly at the bar as they sipped the clouded beer from large glass tankards. The owner was not in sight and the marshal went across to the barman.

'Who was that fella who just looked in, Matt?' he asked as casually as he could manage.

The man shrugged. 'Didn't say, Marshal. Just asked where he could find Ma Edgerton.'

The marshal chewed his lip thoughtfully. 'Did you tell him?' he asked.

7

'Sure did,' the man laughed. 'It ain't no secret, but he didn't look like he needed no laundry doin'. Looked more like he was out to make trouble for someone.'

The marshal squared his shoulders and pulled in his belly.

'Nobody makes trouble in my town,' he said grandly.

One of the old men at the bar nudged his companion before giving the lawman the benefit of a toothless grin.

'Not even Walt Carol?' he asked innocently.

Nathan Harlow froze for a moment before answering. He could remember the man now, and it was not a pleasant memory. He had been a rustler, hold-up man, and bank-robber. It was only recently that he had emerged from the territory prison after a long sentence.

'Not even him,' he said in a slightly unsteady voice.

'You goin' to run him outa town, Marshal?' the other old man asked hopefully.

'Not if he don't cause no trouble. He ain't on any wanted list no more. He's served his time and I ain't aimin' to bring the past against him.'

He felt like asking for a strong drink but decided against it. He was the law in Vane City and the law had to keep its dignity.

'So he's gone round to Ma Edgerton?' he said quietly.

The three men nodded and stood in silence as the marshal left the saloon and walked slowly down the main street to turn right by the grain store.

Ma Edgerton's neat, white-painted house bore a sign that told the town that the widow-woman now plied her trade as a laundress. The marshal eyed the heavy yellow net curtains but could see no movement behind them. There was a small porch fronting the dusty alley and Walt Carol's horse was tied to one of the uprights. The door was closed and Nathan Harlow looked carefully around to see if he was overlooked by any neighbours. There was no sign of movement anywhere and he slipped quietly round the side of the building until he reached the little yard and could see the back door.

There were several strings of washing hanging in the gentle breeze while two large tubs stood deserted nearby. The smell of bleach hung in the air and a cat sat washing itself by one of the tubs.

The lawman crept over to the back door and listened with his ear pressed against the warm panels. He could hear voices from within but they were faint. He moved further along to where a window was open and a newly baked pie lay cooling on the sill. The voices were louder now and he listened avidly.

'—I'd rather have a beer,' Walt Carol was saying peevishly.

'Well, I ain't got no beer so coffee is what you get in this house.' Ma Edgerton's voice was loud and harsh. 'I don't want you nor those no-good brothers of mine comin' here and disturbin' decent folks. What's past is past and I ain't helpin' them no more.'

'Pat'll be mighty sorry to hear that, Ma. He's plannin' to break out of the territory jail in the next few weeks and make the family some money. He wanted me to tell you that him and a few friends is comin' back here to settle things with the Kendrews. When that's done, he plans to rob that nice little bank before takin' off for Mexico. There'll be cash aplenty for all of us and he says as how he'd sure welcome you to go south with him.'

'Landsakes! Was there ever such a bletherer? Lookit, Walt Carol, my no-account brother got what he deserved for thinkin' he could rustle the Kendrews' herd. They was quite right to put him where he is now. He was lucky they didn't just string him and his gang up when they had them instead of gettin' the county sheriff to take 'em away. You go tell him I want none of his doings. He ain't worth a load of mule droppings. And what goes for Pat, goes for Mike and Jamie. They're all worthless.'

'Don't take on like that, Ma,' Walt Carol whined. 'Pat wants that you should be here to help him on this. He's got eight or ten good fellas ready to bust him outa jail and then go after the Kendrew family. When that's done, he aims to come here and raid the bank. What he needs to know is when the bank is carryin' the money for the lumber camp's pay day. You can pick up that sort of information, and I can take it back to him.'

There was a slight bang as though the coffee-pot had been slammed down hard.

'Listen to me, you mangey coyote,' Ma Edgerton shouted, 'I ain't gettin' mixed up in this thing. Them days is over since my Bernie died. I like this town and the folks have treated me decent. As for the Kendrews, the old man passed to the Lord three months back and his sons have sold the spread and moved into town to run the grain store. The folks round here will stand by them if there's shootin', so tell that to Pat with my best wishes for a quick hanging. And now you can get the hell outa here before I put a load of buckshot in your ass.'

There were a few more indistinct words and the marshal backed away from the window. He crept round the side of the house again, drawing his gun as he neared the front where the tethered horse raised its head to stare at him with complete indifference.

He stood at the corner of the building with his eyes on the door. It flew open and Walt Carol emerged, almost pushed through it by Ma Edgerton. She slammed it shut and the man was

11

left standing hesitantly on the porch. Nathan Harlow looked quickly around. There were no witnesses as he levelled the pistol and shot the man through the head.

TWO

Ma Edgerton was the first one on the scene. She had heard the shot, hesitated for a few moments, and then peered fearfully through a window. Walt Carol lay dead on the ground with the marshal standing over him, gun in hand and a satisfied look on his face. Walt's Colt lay a foot or so away from the dead man's hand. It was cocked, ready for use, and his lifeless fingers still seemed to be reaching for the trigger. Ma Edgerton came out on to the porch and stood silently, looking first at the body and then at the triumphant lawman. Neither of them spoke.

The mayor arrived next. He was followed by a crowd of people who filled the narrow lane, pushing and shoving for the best view. Tobias Vane, first citizen of Vane City, was the marshal's cousin. His chubby face was reddened with the effort he had put into running down the street and across to Ma

Edgerton's house. The mayor looked down at the body as the marshal put away his pistol with a modest flourish.

'I tried to take him quietly,' he said in a reasonable voice, 'but these fellas never give up playin' the gunfighter. I don't stand for that sort of thing in my town.'

There was a rumble of agreement from the crowd and one or two hands stretched out to pat Nathan Harlow on the back.

'Quite right,' the mayor snapped. 'Who is he, Nathan?'

'Fella named Walt Carol. Rode with the Bullen gang and has been callin' on Pat Bullen's sister here. I challenged him as he left the house, but the coyote just drew on me. It was one big mistake. He weren't fast enough.'

There was another ripple of approval and the marshal's modest grin thanked them all for their support. The mortician arrived and everybody made way for him and his assistant as they knelt in front of the body.

Mayor Vane waved an imperious hand to move folks back a little. Then he approached the silent Ma Edgerton and ushered her and the marshal into the little house. The mayor sat his short, round frame on the most comfortable chair and smoothed down his ample grey hair with a podgy hand.

'And now, Ma,' he said portentously, 'suppose you

tell me what this Walt Carol fella wanted with you.'

The marshal listened anxiously as she told her story. It was pretty much as he had heard it from the open window and he felt relieved that the town was now being warned of the danger to come.

'Well, I reckon the marshal here can deal with Pat Bullen if he turns up,' Tobias Vane said with a confident smile. 'He's as good a lawman as you can get.'

'I'll need deputies,' Nathan Harlow protested. 'The whole town will have to back me.'

The mayor stood up and straightened his waistcoat.

'And you shall have them if necessary,' he said quietly, 'and all the support you desire. But don't forget, Nathan, Walt Carol ain't goin' back to give any message to Pat Bullen. You stopped that. We'll also be contactin' the prison and the county by telegraph. With what we can tell them, I reckon they'll keep a close eye on the fella.'

'And if they don't?' the lawman asked fearfully.

Tobias Vane shrugged. 'Well, they can at least warn us when he gets loose.'

'And what about this gang he's got organized?'

'They ain't goin' to move if he's still in jail. I figure as how there can be legal reasons to keep him behind bars after this little affair. I'll have a word with lawyer Mason. He's got a legal book somewhere in his office.'

Ma Edgerton snorted. 'Is he sober enough to read it?' she asked.

The mayor frowned. 'Always until late afternoon, ma'am,' he said with dignity. 'He never touches a drop before lunch.'

Nathan Harlow scratched his chin noisily. 'Pat Bullen's got a few years to do yet,' he said thoughtfully. 'They might not add anything to his sentence, and them territory folk is so arrogant that they might figure their jail is good enough to hold him. Maybe there ain't a law to cover this.'

'Well, I'll telegraph the county seat and tell them what's happened,' Mayor Vane said dismissively. 'Surely they can do something for us. I reckon we'd oblige them if the boot was on the other foot.'

'The marshal would come out shooting,' Ma Edgerton said dryly.

Marshal Harlow was the true authentic hero. He strutted around and received the homage of his neighbours with a cheerful and modest smile. They bought him drinks and slapped him on the back. He never hesitated to tell them of how dangerous the late Walt Carol was and how many crimes were listed against him on the old Wanted notices. He was careful never to mention that Walt's gun had never been drawn until the marshal had taken it from the holster after the man was dead.

The mayor telegraphed the county seat as he

had promised, and was assured that Pat Bullen was still safely locked away and that Vane City would be notified as soon as the prison gates opened to turn him loose on an unwelcoming world.

Marshal Harlow was glad to hear the news but still felt an occasional tremor of fear at the thought that Pat Bullen and his gang might one day descend on Vane City. He laid his plans accordingly.

THREE

It was several weeks later, and on a dry, windy day, that J. Samuel Davis came to town. He drove a large wooden wagon that was cheerfully painted in candy stripes and told the world that he sold household goods; all the latest books and magazines, as well as the newest novelties from the great northern cities. His name was there in gold leaf and the two roan horses that drew the rig were adorned with bright brass trimmings and ribbons plaited into their manes.

He was a large, vigorous man in his early fifties; as noticeable as his wagon in the white trail coat, tall hat, and mass of wavy grey hair that peeked out to join the long sideburns that edged his smiling mouth. Smiling was his trade. It persuaded the customers to part with money. And coupled with sweet talk in his fine Southern voice, J. Samuel could charm the rattlesnakes from under their rocks.

People looked at him as he drove down the main street of Vane City. They smiled back without quite knowing why, and Davis waved cheerfully as he brought his rig to a halt outside the office of Marshal Harlow.

After hitching the horses to the rail, J. Samuel strode into the jailhouse with the confident air of a man who does not doubt his welcome. Nathan Harlow looked up from the game of patience he was playing and found himself facing an outstretched hand. It was a warm hand, well manicured, and with a large diamond ring on the middle finger. The marshal looked at it enviously.

'My name is J. Samuel Davis, Marshal,' the visitor said in a grand, theatrical voice, 'and I am passing through your lovely town on my way to the perils of the big city. I mean to stay here for a night or two to rest myself and my animals, and would greatly appreciate directions as to which may be the best hotel.'

The marshal took the hand limply and stared at the visitor for a moment. He got up from the desk and went to peer out of the window.

'You're a drummer,' he said bluntly, 'and you're sellin' the same sort of things we got stores for in this town. I reckon that folk won't like that.'

'My dear Marshal, I shall not offend a living soul.'

Mr Davis took the lawman by the elbow and spoke with great confidentiality.

'The things I sell are not usually to be found outside places like New York, Phoenix, and other fine cities. Novelties, Marshal, for the discerning eye. I will not be harming the local storekeepers in any way, I can assure you. And if I should cause you any problems by the number of folk who gather round my rig, I'm certain we can come to some arrangement to compensate for your time and effort.'

Marshal Harlow looked at the bland face and smiling mouth. His own expression relaxed a little and he crossed to the stove and lifted off the coffee-pot.

'Maybe you'd like to sit down for a few minutes and take a cup,' he said in warmer tones.

'I will be honoured,' J. Samuel replied as he seated himself on a dusty chair.

'Just a day or two, you said?'

'Yes, I am on my way west, but the horses need a rest, and frankly, so do I. One does not get any younger and the weather is as hot as the devil's tongue.'

'It sure is.'

The two men drank their coffee in companionable intimacy. They talked of territory affairs, of the cattle trade, and of life in large cities. When J. Samuel got up to leave, the marshal was wealthier by ten dollars and J. Samuel had the information that he required.

J. Samuel Davis did a good trade once word got around that his rig was tucked away behind the best hotel in town. The Harris House was now the only hotel in town, but the fiction was maintained that the various rooming-houses classified as hotel accommodation.

He was installed in the best room the place could offer, and once settled in, he opened up for business to a steady flow of ladies who wanted the latest magazines and books from the big city. He had fripperies for them too. The newest bonnets from the East and fashionable parasols in attractive colours.

It was early evening before the throng cleared and the drummer prepared to step down from the back of the wagon. As he ducked his head to avoid the low doorway, he found himself looking down at Mayor Tobias Vane. The First Citizen introduced himself in a stiff manner as though suspicious of the man who might be a business rival. The mayor owned the biggest general store in town and he was anxious not to lose custom to some upstart travelling salesman.

'I am delighted to make your acquaintance, Mr Mayor,' J. Samuel said grandly. 'Please step up and take a seat in my little abode.'

The mayor climbed up the wooden steps and

found himself in a large area that was packed with merchandise. Beyond it was a small space where a narrow bunk-bed lay across the width of the wagon. The bed was neatly made up and a large tin trunk lay beneath it with J. Samuel's initials outlined in gold under the brass lock. The place smelled fresh and all his personal belongings were neatly stacked.

'I live here when on the move,' the drummer explained, 'but after a long journey, it is a relief to stay at a hotel and enjoy the privilege of somebody else doing the cooking. I really miss my late dear wife.'

He was reaching into a small cupboard as he spoke, pulling out a bottle of good whiskey and a couple of glasses. He gestured the mayor to sit on the edge of the bed while he took the small stool. The two men raised their glasses before drinking the aromatic spirit.

'A good whiskey,' the mayor said appreciatively.

The drummer sighed. 'The last of it, I'm sorry to tell you,' he said with nostalgia in his voice. 'The days of buying the best are now over for me, I'm afraid. That is why I am reduced to this.'

He waved his beringed hand around the wagon. The large diamond shone brilliantly in the dimness as he poured another drink.

'You don't seem to be sellin' much in my line,' Tobias conceded with a certain relief in his voice.

'Indeed not,' J. Samuel assured him. 'I specialize in novelties. It's safer that way and nobody is offended. But it is a hard way to make a living when one has seen better days.'

'What did you do before this, then?'

'Ah, you might well ask, sir. I was a landowner, growing cotton and owning two hundred slaves. The war finished me, sir. My land is gone, my house destroyed, and my poor wife has passed away in straitened circumstances. Another casualty of war.'

The mayor nodded with sudden gloom. 'We all suffered to some degree,' he said wistfully. 'I lost a brother fightin' at first Manassas. Not twenty years old was poor Henry. My father started this town before the war and it flourished in the goldrush days. Then the ore petered out and the war took away so much – we never quite seemed to recover. Them Yankees have a lot to answer for.'

He glanced round the little place and his eyes lighted on a framed daguerreotype that hung from one of the wooden walls.

'Ain't that our president?' he asked solemnly.

J. Samuel heaved a sigh and nodded his head. 'It is indeed,' he said sadly, 'and only here in the South would I have it on display. Uncle Jeff deserved better, poor man.'

The drummer's beringed hand was resting on two new-looking books on which the titles were clearly to be seen. Mayor Vane reached out and touched one of them with awe.

'Them's the books that he wrote,' he said quietly.

'Indeed they are, and signed by him as you see.'

J. Samuel opened one of the volumes and passed it to the First Citizen. The scrawl of ex-president Jefferson Davis was there, and it was a dedication to his beloved nephew, J. Samuel Davis.

The mayor began to sweat in the heat of the wagon. His hand trembled as he held the book like some precious relic. He caressed it and scanned the title avidly: *Rise and Fall of the Confederate Government* in two volumes, and just off the press.

'You're his nephew,' he murmured in admiration.

'I have that honour. His brother Tom was my father. Older than him, of course, and dead these past five years.'

'Do you ever see him?'

'I visited him in New Orleans when those damned Yankees let him out of prison. His health isn't good. We're a broken family now.'

'I can believe it.' The mayor shook his head sadly.

J. Samuel poured out some more whiskey. He raised his glass.

'To the Confederacy,' he said softly as the two men drank. The drummer heaved a deep sigh as he downed the fine-quality liquor.

'I looked in on some old friends of the family on my way here,' he murmured, 'but time seems to have overtaken them with equal cruelty. There are new people on their spread. With accents more Northern than I really care to hear.'

'Who would they be?' the mayor asked in a slightly fuddled voice.

'The Kendrews. Sold up and moved on, so the incomers told me.'

The mayor nodded. 'That's right. The old man died some time back and his two sons moved into town. They bought Willy Mitchell's grain store. If you want to see them, it's just at the south end of the main street, down on the right.'

'Good, I must call on them. They won't remember me, but their father was a friend of the family. I'll at least convey my belated respects to his memory.'

'And where will you be travellin' next, Mr Davis?' the mayor asked.

The other man looked a little sheepish. Then he seemed to make up his mind.

'For the benefit of the town, I'm on my way round the territory. Doing a roaring trade as usual. The truth, just between a couple of old Confederate supporters, is that I'm heading for a big place where I'm going to sell one or two family heirlooms for the best price I can get. It's humiliating but I have my daughters to think of. They're nearing marriageable age, and these things cost money.' He shrugged. 'The devil drives hard when a family man has his duty to do.'

25

He raised a hand and looked wistfully at the large diamond ring on his chubby finger.

'I shall miss this,' he said. 'It's been in the family for three generations, but now it has to go.'

'It must be rather valuable.'

'I believe so. That's why I need a big city where there are folk who can afford to purchase such things.'

'How much – er – would it be worth?'

'In a store I can imagine it fetching more than a thousand dollars. But life being what it is, I shall consider myself a very fortunate man to get half that. I was hoping to pass it on to my elder child, but....'

He sighed and reached out his hand to pick up a small mirror set in an ivory frame. He passed the diamond across it with a harsh scraping sound and left a thin, clean line on the glass.

'Purest of the pure,' he said in his deep, theatrical voice. 'I will surely miss Grandma's ring.'

'A very elegant stone,' the mayor agreed breathlessly, 'and with a distinguished ancestry. My wife has a birthday soon and I would like to do something special for that day. A memory of meeting a Jefferson. I – I could manage five hundred dollars.'

J. Samuel looked hard at the man as though fearful that he might be the victim of some cruel joke.

'My dear sir,' he said with deep emotion, 'you are

my saviour! The prospect of going into some city store and haggling would be more than I could bear. It is yours, dear sir. Here, take it now.'

He began to tug the ring from his finger while the mayor assured him there was no need to hurry.

'No, no. I must go to the bank first,' he protested. 'I don't keep that sort of money around the house. I shall collect five hundred dollars first thing in the morning and will be honoured to own a ring that has adorned the hands of the Jefferson family.'

'You speak graciously, sir. Have you a good bank in this town then?'

'Fair enough. Lackin' in prosperity since the gold went, but still active.'

The drummer's innocent eyes took on a slightly harder look.

'I have heard that there are some very good timber businesses in the neighbourhood,' he said casually. 'So with them, and the local stores and ranches, it must keep things pretty busy. There is only one saloon, I notice, but Saturday nights should be rather lively.'

'Oh, we're recoverin' slowly but surely. This town will be big again one day. Timber-workers and farmers are a lot quieter than gold-miners, but we still have some rare Saturday nights. Once in a while.'

'So Saturday nights are quieter now? I will get some sleep then?'

'Any three weekends out of four. The timber companies arrive once a month to collect the wages. Then their hands come in to spend the money on the Saturday. You'll get some sleep tonight. The next pay day is two weeks away. They collect from the bank on Thursdays and pay them Saturday noon. After that it's a full night for the Golden Horse.'

J. Samuel smiled benignly and poured another drink to finish off the bottle.

The mayor left a short time later, reeling slightly but in a very happy state of mind. He had been presented with a signed daguerreotype of President Jefferson Davis, and he had made a deal on a diamond ring that would be the talk of Vane City.

J. Samuel was even happier than the mayor. He sat in the wagon, tugging the ring off his finger and wrapping it in a piece of clean white linen. He tucked this securely into one of his pockets while from another he took out an identical-looking ring which bore a large white sapphire that was worth all of thirty dollars. It fitted snugly on his finger and glittered treacherously in the fading daylight.

FOUR

Nathan Harlow was asleep in his office chair. The large belly heaved gently as he snored through the late afternoon with an empty coffee-cup in front of him and a greasy plate that two roaches were exploring with interest.

The opening of the door dragged him unpleasantly awake as it slammed back against the wall and sent the roaches scampering for safer parts. It was the mayor, his face dark with anger and his short, rotund body quivering with emotion.

'What time did that drummer fella leave town?' he snapped as the marshal straightened up behind the desk.

'The drummer? Oh, some time after noon, I guess.' Nathan pulled out a silver watch and squinted closely at the dial. 'It would be nigh on four hours ago. Why? What in hell's troublin' you, Tobias?'

'Then he can't have got far. Get yo'self after him and bring the fella back to town with my money. And I don't want no excuses. I want that Davis fella in the jailhouse before the night's out.'

'What for? I can't go around arrestin' folk without a reason, Tobias. What's he done?'

'Done!' The mayor took a deep breath. 'He posed as a Southern gentleman and swindled me outa five hundred dollars. That's what he's done. So get yo'self to horse and collar him.'

'Now, lookit, Tobias, he could have gone in any direction and he's had four hours' start. I just can't go gallopin' off like some mad general...!'

'Which way was he headin' when he left town?'

'He was headin' north, I reckon.'

'Then you head north. He's got a big wagon drawn by two horses, so he should be easy to follow. He'll leave a trail a mile wide, and he's got to stop at night. Now, don't stand there arguin' the point. Get saddled up and move your ass outa here. I want my money back.'

The marshal reluctantly did as his cousin ordered, and was chivvied all the while he saddled and brought his mare out of the corral behind the jailhouse. Even when he was mounted and ready to go, Tobias was still complaining bitterly that the marshal should even have considered letting a drummer enter Vane City and have a chance to cheat honest folk of their hard-earned cash.

'And bring that fella back dead or alive,' he was ordered. 'And Nathan, that drummer is carryin' my money, and somethin' else that's also rightly mine. I don't want any mistakes about this. You get back everything I'm entitled to.'

The marshal looked down from the height of the saddle. His eyes were wary.

'And what's all this about?' he asked with sudden boldness. 'You sure is as excited as hell over a few dollars.'

'Five hundred is not a few dollars, and never mind what it's all about. Just make certain sure that I see everythin' he has on that wagon of his.'

The lawman nodded and turned his animal towards the main street. The mayor suddenly had second thoughts and scampered after him.

'Nathan,' he whispered urgently. 'I got me a better idea.'

He grabbed the bridle of the marshal's horse and looked around to make sure that nobody could overhear.

'There ain't really no need to bring him back to town,' he said quietly. 'If he should choose to shoot it out, all the stuff on that wagon would be lookin' for a new owner. Get my meaning?'

The marshal grinned slightly. 'I would be reckonin' on that bein' two new owners,' he said firmly.

'That's what I have in mind. And, Nathan, this is important to me. If you don't catch up with him,

31

Vane City might be lookin' for a new marshal.'

The lawman swung his horse jubilantly towards the north end of town and went galloping off to do his duty. The mayor watched for a few moments and then walked hurriedly back to his store.

There were a few customers there and his daughter was serving one of them while his wife supervised from the cash desk. A young man was unpacking a wooden case of yellow soap and the mayor called him urgently.

'I got me a little job for you, Will,' he said as he took him out of hearing. 'Go saddle your horse and put on your gun. Take my Winchester as well and pack a little food.'

'What's it all about, Uncle Tobias?' the youth asked.

'Never mind that now. Just get saddled up and I'll tell you when you're ready to go. Hurry up, lad. You've got a trail to follow.'

Will Vane was a tall youth with wheat-coloured hair and a frank, clear face that flashed a certain honesty of character. He was the only son of the mayor's elder brother who had died during the war. Will was bright, hard-working, and Tobias Vane employed him for a pittance about the store.

He brought his horse round to the front a few minutes later and the mayor leaned over the hitching rail to have a quiet word with him.

'Cousin Nathan has just left town after that

32

drummer fella who cheated me,' he said urgently. 'I want you to ride along and see that everythin' goes right. I want what's mine, so make sure that Nathan brings back that wagon and every bit of merchandise in it. I don't want that crooked barrel of hogwash pocketin' nothing that I should be seeing. Your job is to look after my interests. You understand that, boy?'

'Yes, Uncle Tobias,' the lad said as he mounted. 'But Uncle Nathan is – family, and he's the marshal. He wouldn' cheat you, would he?'

The mayor snorted with derision. 'Take my advice, lad. Never make the mistake of trustin' your kin where cash money's concerned. Nathan has sticky fingers and he don't live on just a lawman's pay. Now, get yourself on his trail and don't lose sight of him or that drummer.'

He slapped the lad's horse on its sturdy rump and sent the animal galloping off in the direction the marshal had taken a short time before.

Nathan Harlow rode through the hot dryness of the scrubland with his eyes fixed on the deep ruts made by the wagon. The drummer had left easy signs to follow and the marshal had little doubt that he would catch up with him in an hour or so.

What would happen then was something that worried him. J. Samuel Davis may have looked like some soft city fella but he carried a four-barrelled

Sharps derringer in his pocket, and the marshal had caught a glimpse of it. He was already planning how to deal with the situation. He would wait until it was dark and then kill the man while he sat at his fire or slept in the wagon. It was the easiest way. And the safest.

He could guess where the drummer would camp for the night. There was a stream that ran down from the distant hills and joined the San Pedro river some miles further west. It was a shallow flow of water, but pure and cool in the hot summer of the lower pastures. He slowed his pace as he neared it, and finally halted just as the last rays of the sun vanished over the horizon.

Marshal Harlow checked his guns, tethered his mount near some decent patches of grass, and then started off on foot. He had carefully taken off his spurs to move slowly and with a slight feeling of trepidation along the rutted trail in the gathering darkness.

There was a sudden noise behind him and he swung round nervously. Young Will Vane was dismounting from his horse and tethering it to the same low branch that the marshal had used. Nathan raised a slightly trembling finger to his lips and hurried back to join the new arrival.

'What the hell in tarnation is you here for, boy?' he demanded angrily. 'I got serious work to do here and the last blame thing I need is for some greenhorn whippersnapper buttin' in and spoilin' things.'

Will Vane grinned in the darkness.

'Uncle Tobias sent me,' he said quietly. 'Told me to keep an eye out for his interests.'

'That goddamned little crook don't trust nobody,' the marshal snapped. 'Well, I don't trust him neither. Tobias is as twisted as a coiled rattlesnake. You should know that, lad. You work for the bastard.'

'What do you want me to do, Uncle Nathan?'

'Well, I'll tell you, boy. This drummer fella is armed. He ain't the pantywaist he looks, and I reckon him for a shootin' man. So I aim to play it safe and kill him afore he kills me. That's what law enforcement is all about.'

'You ain't goin' to try and arrest him?'

The marshal winked in the darkness and almost managed a grin.

'Hell, no,' he chuckled. 'I figure that our mayor would be right displeased if I was to take the pedlar back to town alive. A trial's a sort of public thing, and if Tobias was swindled by this fella, he wouldn't want folk to know how he'd been taken for one real fool rube. So we go in there ready for shootin', and as soon as he makes for a gun, we open fire. Safest and surest way, lad. You with me?'

'Yes, Uncle Nathan.'

'Right. Then get them spurs off and let's move

quiet-like until we find out where's he's makin' camp for the night.'

He led the way through the stumpy grass, edging along the bank of the stream until the wagon came in sight. The two heavy horses were nearby, shorn of their harness and munching gently on the fresh vegetation by the water's sloping edge. Shadows flitted against the sides of the rig as a fire burned warmly nearby while the smell of coffee and bacon lingered in the air.

J. Samuel Davis kneeled in front of the fire, stirring the grounds in an enamel coffee-pot while he whistled softly to himself. He was hatless, his whitened hair like a halo against the flames and his hand bearing the large diamond ring that winked in the flickering light.

If Will Vane had not been there, the marshal would happily have shot the drummer in the back. It would have been so easy and he would then have pocketed everything of value that he could find. Tobias would only get what was due to him. Nathan Harlow would be the hero, and would take his reward. He pulled a face and stepped forward with his pistol levelled.

'Just get to your feet, quiet-like,' he snapped in his best official voice. 'We got some business to tend here.'

The man stood up slowly and turned to calmly face the marshal and his companion.

'I rather thought it would be you,' he said quietly, 'and you've brought a friend as well. Take a seat, Marshal, and share a bit of supper with me. There's plenty for all.'

The lawman frowned. 'You heard us coming?' he growled angrily.

J. Samuel smiled benignly. 'As delicate as a troop of cavalry. This is your deputy, I take it?'

'No, just some young fella along for the ride.'

'Ah, then what brings you on this long journey from town? I thought we'd made a financial agreement.'

Nathan Harlow bit his lips and turned to Will Vane.

'You go put the harness on them horses, lad,' he ordered. 'We'll be takin' that wagon back to Vane City.'

The young man nodded and went to carry out his orders. He was well out of earshot when the marshal turned back to answer J. Samuel's question.

'I got me a kinda problem,' he explained a little sheepishly. 'The mayor reckons as how you flim-flammed him and he ain't any too pleased about it. He says that I gotta take you and your rig back to town. He's also my kin, so I got no choice.'

The man shrugged. 'Marshal,' he said smilingly, 'I paid you good money to let me trade back there. All you have to do now is to return and tell the mayor that you lost track of me. I won't be saying anything different.'

Nathan shook his head. 'It ain't that simple, fella. I gotta take you in. One way or another.'

The smile died on the drummer's face and his right hand stole towards the trail coat pocket. The ring winked in the firelight as it moved nearer the hidden derringer.

'I think you're making a mistake, Marshal,' he said quietly. 'When I mention to the mayor that you were bribed to let me trade in his town, I reckon that you'll be out of a job. Why can't we just part peacefully?'

'I'd like that, fella,' Nathan grinned. 'I really would like it. But if I don't do what I set out to do, I'll lose my job anyway. The mayor is real annoyed about this business.'

There was a long silence between the two men while only the sound of Will Vane harnessing the horses disturbed the evening air.

The drummer eventually threw his hands wide in a gesture of resignation. 'Well, I suppose I have no choice,' he said sadly, 'but I do feel you're making a grave error.'

He turned to the fire, removed the coffee-pot, and began to kick sand over the sparkling flames. His trail coat blew wide open in the gentle, warm breeze as he used that moment to draw the derringer and cock it.

He swung round and fired, but two more shots disturbed the night air and the horses neighed and pawed the ground in noisy fright.

J. Samuel Davis stood for a moment with an expression of surprise on his handsome face. Then he slowly fell to his knees, swaying backwards into the dying flames. His weight smothered them, and after a little twitching, his ponderous body lay still.

'I sure as hell put an end to that one,' the marshal said with grim satisfaction. 'I reckon Tobias will be pleased with the way things turned out.

He slipped the Colt back into its holster without even noticing that Will Vane had already holstered his own gun after neatly shooting the drummer clean through the chest after the marshal's panicky shot went wide.

FIVE

It was close to five in the morning when Will Vane entered town with his strong hands guiding the two horses that pulled the large wagon. His own animal was following on a long tether while Marshal Harlow rode like some triumphant warrior returning from battle. The wagon contained the body of J. Samuel Davis who lay among his dry goods covered by the white trail coat.

The main street was lit only by a hint of dawn in a cloudless sky that heralded another hot day. A few lights shone in the windows of those who had to rise early for work but few people were about and they showed no curiosity until the rig stopped outside the mortician's office. Will Vane was the one who had to bang on the door and shout up at the window. It was a few minutes before the owner appeared, hastily dressed and eager to help carry the body into his parlour.

A few people were gathering now and the marshal modestly told them how he had fought it out with the drummer who had resisted arrest. No mention was made of the part the mayor had played, but Nathan Harlow was happy to tell the folks that the man was a flim-flam artist and that their brave lawman had called him to account. It went down well, particularly because some of the local men had bought books that were supposed to be highly erotic. They had been very disappointed at the insipid contents for which they had paid treble the real market price. Nathan was once again a hero.

The wagon was taken round to the rear of the jailhouse where the draught horses were penned with the marshal's own animals. A hastily dressed mayor arrived, hurrying across the rutted main street to join the lawman and young Will by the corral. He wasted no time with idle pleasantries.

'Did you search the body?' he asked anxiously.

Nathan Harlow looked at him with contempt and made a slight gesture with his eyes in the direction of Will Vane. The mayor took the hint.

'You done a good job, boy,' he said in as jovial a voice as he could muster. 'Go get yo'self some rest. You have a full day's work ahead.'

The young man nodded and left silently for his lodging over the mayor's rear storeroom. The two men watched him disappear round the corner before speaking again.

'He went for his gun,' Nathan Harlow said, 'and we shot it out. The boy let off a round or two as well, but he just got in the way. I didn't need no help, Tobias. Sendin' him after me was a fool thing to do.'

The mayor was not interested in the marshal's opinion.

'Well, where's his stuff?' he snapped angrily. 'Let me see it all.'

'It's here in a sack across my saddle. He had twenty dollars on him and a gold watch.'

As the marshal reached up to remove the sack from the crupper the sharp point of a knife dug into his ribs. He let out a yell of fright and the animal shied as he staggered against its flank.

'You play tricks like that on me, Nathan Harlow, and kin or no kin, I'll skewer your rotten hide to a barn door.' The mayor's voice was harsh and deadly as he took off the pressure and lowered the blade to his side.

The marshal swallowed noisily. 'There weren't no call for that, Tobias. I ain't finished tellin' you.'

He rubbed the small gash in his chest. 'There was also five hundred dollars in new notes,' he said mournfully.

'My five hundred dollars, you fool jackass! Why the hell did I send you after him?'

'It's all safe and sound,' the marshal whined. 'Let's go into the office.'

They entered the shabby room and Nathan lit the oil-lamp with a shaky hand. The mayor had tucked the knife away inside his coat and was waiting impatiently for the lawman to empty the little sack of loot on to the desk.

A jumble of things fell out. There were a few banknotes, a clatter of small coins, and a large watch and chain that were of good quality gold. There was a small black-backed notebook, a silver pencil, and a tiny white cotton bag with a cluster of rings that bore large stones. The mayor seized them with such haste that the marshal eyed him suspiciously.

'Where's my money?' Tobias Vane snapped angrily.

The marshal reached reluctantly into his back pocket and produced a bundle of notes.

'Just keepin' it safe,' he said sheepishly. 'What did you give that fella five hundred dollars for?'

'Never you mind. There was a ring on his finger. Where's that gone?'

The lawman made another reluctant dive for his waistcoat pocket to produce a ring identical to those that had been in the little white bag. The mayor snatched it from him.

'Now, I'll tell you how we handle this, Nathan,' he said in a calmer voice. 'I'll go through his goods and see what can be sold in the store. Everything else can be auctioned off by Ned Tinker. After his funeral expenses are paid, we divide what's left over between us.'

'That goes for the horses and rig as well?'

'Sure does. We deserve a little profit outa that jackal.'

'That leaves the rings,' the marshal said with sudden bravery. 'What about them?'

'What about them?'

'Ain't they bein' auctioned off?'

Tobias Vane was silent for a moment. Then he put a gentle and confident hand on the marshal's arm.

'Nathan,' he said quietly, 'you and me is kin and I can say to you what I can't say to other folk. Private things – like how I was took by a smart drummer. I wouldn't like it spread round the town that the mayor fell for a piece of flap-doodlin' that shouldn't have fooled a man of my experience. I made an ass of myself but I don't want the whole town to know about it.'

He shook his head sadly at his own cupidity and the marshal listened with wide-open mouth as the tale unfolded.

'He said that he was a good Southerner and kin to President Jefferson Davis. Even had a picture of him, and books signed by him. Told me that them rings was family heirlooms, and that he needed ready cash. Well, it's Martha's birthday soon, and I figured on what a treat it would be for her to have the biggest diamond ring in town. She's been a good wife to me, and I reckon that's what put me off my guard. I paid him five hundred dollars for one of them rings. He even let me chose the one I wanted. They're all some cheap stone. Maybe even glass. So I aim to put them away some place where no other fool like this old fool will pay good money for them.'

'You sure was took, Tobias,' the marshal said in wonderment. 'But don't fret on it. I ain't the gossipin' kind.'

'Good man. Now, let's light that stove and have us a nice cup of coffee with a little extra somethin' for celebration.'

The marshal's deep-set eyes took on a slightly cunning look.

''That fella had a lotta good shirts and pants, Tobias,' he said. 'I reckon as how they'd fit me right well....'

The mayor waved a magnanimous hand. 'Shame to waste them, cousin. You take all his linen.'

The brightness of the day brought a new fame to Marshal Harlow. He strutted round the town, telling all who cared to hear about his gunfight with the drummer who had swindled the poor folk of Vane City. He was slapped on the back, congratulated, and ended up in the saloon taking a few early drinks from all who were willing to offer.

Tobias looked across the street at what was happening. He peered out cynically through the window of his store as the lawman paraded himself like some modest conqueror for all to admire. Will Vane was sweeping out the back room when his uncle entered and closed the door carefully behind him.

'Now, lad,' he said in a fatherly tone, 'tell me what really happened last night.'

The young man stopped work and related the story in a simple, unvarnished manner.

'I see.' The mayor pulled out a small cigar and lit it. 'So cousin Nathan did the shooting. Is that right?'

'I guess so.'

'Did you fire?'

The youth hesitated for a moment. 'I got off one shot,' he admitted.

'And what did you hit?'

'Uncle Nathan reckons I didn't hit nothing.'

The man smiled. 'Is that a fact now? And what do you reckon?'

'I reckon I ain't arguin' with nobody, Uncle Tobias. He's the marshal.'

'It's a wise man who knows when to keep his mouth shut.' The mayor handed over two silver dollars and dropped some ash on the clean floor. 'I'll tell you something, lad,' he said bluntly. 'My cousin Nathan is one almighty boastful man. But I got my

46

own opinion about who killed the drummer.'

He left the room with a smile on his face and nodded cheerily to a couple of customers as they paid at the cash desk.

It was only when he was back upstairs in the living-quarters that he took out the little bag of rings from his waistcoat pocket. He weighed them in his hand, still smiling as he considered where best to dump them where they would never be found. He had already scored the bedroom mirror with a fine sharp line from the real diamond ring. That was now in his safe where it would remain with the recovered $500. The mayor was a happy man.

A couple of hours passed before he remembered the notebook that had been among J. Samuel's effects. He put down the journal he was reading and crossed to the mahogany dresser on which it lay with the silver pencil and gold watch.

It was a small book with a black leather binding and a little loop for the silver pencil to be safely housed. He opened it at random and his face tightened as he read the contents.

'Old Kendrew is dead,' he mouthed softly, 'and his sons have bought a grain store in Vane City. Pat's sister will not help and Walt Carol had a run-in with the marshal and got himself shot. The local timber company pays out on the third Saturday of each month. The mayor let drop that the cash arrives in town with a heavy escort three days earlier. The banker lives in a brick house just behind the church.'

Tobias Vane started sweating as he tremblingly closed the little book. J. Samuel Davis had been more than a drummer. He was gathering information for Pat Bullen. He stood for a few moments, wondering how to cope with the situation. Then he wiped his brow with a shaky hand and went downstairs again.,

Will Vane was in the backyard drawing water from the iron pump. The mayor took a deep breath to control his voice as he approached the young man.

'I got me an idea, Will lad,' he said cheerfully. 'We really need a deputy marshal in this town, and I figure as you're the man for the job. How about it?'

His nephew stopped pumping up the water to stare at his uncle with a look of quiet astonishment on his face.

'What about Uncle Nathan?' he asked. 'Has he agreed?'

Tobias shrugged. 'Nathan will do as he's told,' he said grandly. 'I'm the mayor and the councilmen will all side with me. You'll get some pay out of it, and still be able to fill in your spare time by workin' for me. There'll be no call for idle hands. The deputy's job is only a part-time one. It's just that I don't trust Cousin Nathan, and you're as honest a fella as I could wish for the job. You'll take over full-time when he retires, or gets fired.'

The youth looked at the mayor's smiling face with a certain reserve.

'You wouldn't be expectin' any sort of trouble, Uncle Tobias?' he asked quietly.

'Bless you! No, lad. This town's as quiet as quiet. But we gotta think of a future for you. Tendin' store ain't a lifetime job for a fella what can ride and shoot.'

The mayor came closer to his nephew and lowered his voice.

'I need someone I can trust around the jailhouse. Nathan ain't an honest man, as you may have guessed, and I have to look after the interests of the town. He tried cheatin' me over this drummer business. Pocketed some of the money that was swindled out of folk like me. He needs watchin', boy, and that's your job.'

The mayor went back to his own quarters above the store. He was content with his day's work. He would get his nephew on the town payroll, make a big profit from the death of J. Samuel Davis, and have somebody around the jailhouse to keep a wary eye on Cousin Nathan.

Two weeks passed quietly and the mayor was spending an afternoon in his office at the back of the store. He had brought his bookkeeping up to date and was dropping off to sleep when a sudden knock on the door panel jarred him wide awake again. He got up from the chair to see who it was. The town telegraphist stood there; a little man with a shock of grey hair and silver-rimmed spectacles that fell forward on his button nose.

'I got a message for you, Mr Mayor,' he said eagerly. He held out a flimsy piece of paper and the First Citizen felt in his waistcoat pocket for his own glasses. He adjusted them carefully to read the message.

Pat Bullen had escaped from the territory jail after killing two guards. It happened at night and nobody knew where he was or how many people had helped him to get away.

SIX

The ranch was a small one by local standards. Rich pasture ran along the river banks but was dry and sparse as it neared the low foothills that were crowned in a vague mist. The heat of the day had driven the cattle towards the welcoming water and in the far distance the low ranch-house lay, white and red-tiled on a slight plateau.

The group of riders was moving at great speed, ten or twelve of them spreading out to approach the buildings on all sides. They were rough-looking men, well armed and with many days of beard growing on their dust-covered faces.

A woman came out of the ranch-house, carrying a shotgun and waiting nervously to see what they were going to do. A small boy peered through the window, his face white against the glass. She aimed the weapon at the man who seemed to be the leader and who rode a pale cow pony that slavered

51

foam as it was brought to a halt at her doorway.

'What do you want?' she shouted angrily. 'You got no business here.'

The man on the pale horse took off his hat to wipe the dark brow. He was thin, with high cheekbones and a narrow mouth below a large beak of a nose.

'I want Ted Kendrew,' he said grimly. 'Where's he hiding?'

The woman stared at him silently for a moment.

'Ted Kendrew?' The name seemed to mean nothing to her. Then she recalled it. 'Oh, he died way back,' she said. 'We bought the ranch from his sons. What would you be wantin' him for?'

'Where are his sons?' the man asked without answering her question.

'They bought a grain store in Vane City. Had enough of ranchin', I reckon.'

The leader glanced round at his followers. He seemed uncertain of what to do next. He turned in the saddle to view the pasture around the ranch-house.

'You got plenty of hired help?' he asked in a quieter voice.

'Enough, and all in range of a holler.'

As if to bear out what she said, two horsemen appeared from behind a clump of trees and increased their pace when they saw the strangers. One of them let out a series of shrill whistles and another man came over a small ridge, swinging his horse in the direction of the signal.

'We ain't lookin' for trouble,' the stranger explained hurriedly, 'but we got things to settle with the Kendrew family.'

'Then go settle it, fella,' the woman said with increasing confidence. 'Don't come around here makin' trouble for peaceful folk.'

Another man had appeared, wielding an old army rifle. He stood in the doorway of a shed, viewing the strangers with open hostility.

'We'll be on our way,' their leader said flatly. 'Don't intend to cause no trouble, ma'am.'

He made a gesture of farewell and spun his horse to lead the riders away from the house. The owners of the ranch watched until the group of horsemen was out of sight and the cloud of dust began to settle again.

'So what was all that about?' the man who had stood near the shed asked anxiously.

The woman told him and he chewed thoughtfully on his lip as he thought about it.

'Well, we never knew the Kendrews,' he said quietly, 'but I reckon it would be right neighbourly for me to ride into town and warn them young fellas that they got trouble ahead of them.'

'I think that would be a good thing, Pa,' the woman agreed. 'Make sure you keep out of sight, though. They were a mighty rough-lookin' bunch.'

He nodded, 'I'll go by way of the creek,' he said, 'and have a word with the marshal while I'm at it. He won't like a crowd of roughnecks makin' trouble in his town.'

The group of horsemen stopped a couple of miles further on to water their tired horses. The animals were winded after the long and hasty journey from where they had broken Pat Bullen out of jail. Two of the gang had been killed, but they had done their share of fighting, and their boss was free to lead them to revenge on the Kendrews and to some wealth in Vane City.

One of them drew closer to Pat Bullen. He leaned over the saddle confidentially as the horses drank.

'We coulda taken that ranch, Pat,' he said softly. 'The fellas are wonderin' why you didn't turn 'em loose.'

The leader gave a tight grin. 'Once we knew the Kendrews wasn't there, what'd be the point? We can't go stealin' cattle until after we've dealt with Vane City. And if we get that bank cleaned out, we won't be needin' cattle.'

'That's another thing, boss. Your brother Mike tells me that Walt Carol never got a message back to you. Neither did some drummer fella. Do we know when there'll be real big money in the bank?'

Pat Bullen ground his teeth and tried to be patient.

'Somethin' went wrong, I reckon,' he said in as calm a voice as he could muster. 'We just gotta take what's there and be thankful. Vane City is an easy place to deal with. The marshal is a fat coward and the rest of 'em ain't much better. We'll ride in at night, burn down the grain store and kill the Kendrew brothers. Then we round up the bank fella and make him open up.'

He looked round for his two brothers. Mike was down at the edge of the stream, rinsing his sweaty face, while the eldest of the Bullens was sitting quietly on his horse chewing tobacco. Pat called them over to him.

'That ranch we just left,' he said quietly, 'ain't worth taking. We got bigger things to do. So don't go talkin' your fool heads off about how I'm runnin' things.'

The two men, stouter editions of himself and with the same narrow mouths, looked sheepish.

'Now, I gotta job for you. The folks at that ranch might have sent somebody into town to warn them that we're on our way. Take your spare horses and head for Vane City pronto. And I mean real fast. Stop anybody who looks like he's carryin' a message to the Kendrews – or the marshal.'

'Do we kill him, Pat?' the eldest brother asked.

'No, you ask him to go prospectin' in California, of course you kill him. Then wait on the edge of town until the rest of us get there. We won't go in until after dark. Now, get moving.'

Mike and Jamie Bullen changed horses and set out at a fast pace in the direction of Vane City. They kept to the high ground wherever possible so that they could see any other horseman in the distance. It was over an hour later that Mike spotted some dust on the horizon and pointed it out to his brother. The two men spurred their horses to catch up with the rider. They came off the high ground now, dipping down a slope where their own dust would be less likely to be seen. They managed a parallel course with their victim, and when they calculated that they were within shooting distance, split up to take him on either flank.

The rider finally saw them and urged his horse faster. He was moving along the banks of a sluggish creek and the ground was soft beneath the hoofs of the tiring animal. He dug in the spurs but got little extra response.

The Bullen brothers were getting closer and Mike tried a few shots with his Colt .44. They went wide but the man being pursued was not used to gunfire directed at him. He ducked low in the saddle, caught his mouth against the animal's neck, and felt his teeth cut through the lower lip. He reeled backwards for a moment, lost control of the horse and almost lost his seat as well. The animal stumbled on the muddy ground, and before he could gather up the reins again, it slipped sideways and he came down in the shallow, muddy creek.

He heard the yell of triumph from close by and pulled his gun from its holster with wet fingers that slipped on the smooth wooden butt. He scrambled to his feet to confront his pursuers and found that they were only yards away.

Two shots split the air, and before he could return fire, the man was staggering backwards with a wound in his left shoulder and another in the chest. He sank slowly into the creek and the water reddened as he died there.

SEVEN

Vane City lay before them bathed in deep shadows as the sun went down over the far hills. The horsemen on the long ride could see the people moving along the main street and in the few side lanes that lay around and behind the stores and corrals. It was a peaceful sight that Pat Bullen and his gang watched with greed written all over their unshaven faces.

Mike leaned over to speak softly to his brother.

'Suppose they're waitin' for us, Pat?' he asked a little fearfully. 'We could be walkin' straight into a trap.'

Pat snorted impatiently. 'Not likely. They don't know nothin' and you took care of that fella from the ranch.'

'The telegraph might have been used though. They could be just plannin' to bushwhack us down there.'

Jamie nodded agreement. Now that they were so close to the town, the other two Bullens were not quite so certain about the outcome. They had helped Pat to escape, but the sight of Vane City was bringing a little reality into their way of thinking. They were getting scared, and it showed.

'Lookit, you two old women,' Pat snarled angrily. 'Nobody knows that we are headin' for Vane City. We moved north after leavin' the territory jail and our trail was easy to follow. Then we turned off through the Oka Valley. We covered up that trail and any posse would have lost us at that point. They'll be searchin' all over now and Vane City is as safe a target as any other. We gotta have money and it's down there in that bank. It's too bad we don't know the best day to move in, but we can't be particular right now.'

He looked at them with contempt.

'I'm one vengeful man,' he said grimly, 'and I aim to kill them Kendrews wherever they are. If we're goin' to do that, we might as well take the bank at the same time. It makes sense. Then we can go south and across the border for a bit of high living. Got any better ideas?'

They had none but still looked worried.

'Now, here's how we play it,' Pat went on, including the other men in the conversation. 'We wait until about midnight when most of the folks will be home in bed. We move in round the back of the town, locate the grain store and break in. Mike and me will do that. Once we're inside, we'll deal with the Kendrews and set the place afire. Jamie will go find some fella and beat the hell out of him until he tells where the banker's living. Then Jamie goes to the banker's house and gets the keys.'

He looked at each of his brothers to make sure they were taking in everything that was said. Jamie was mouthing the orders in an effort to remember them better.

'And, Jamie,' Pat said carefully, 'just make sure that anybody you deal with ain't conscious enough to raise the alarm.'

'I'll kill 'em, Pat. Don't worry.'

The leader heaved a heavy sigh. 'I do worry,' he said bleakly. 'If you go shootin' folks before we've even got into the bank, the whole thing will be over. Just tap 'em on the head with your gun. Now, the rest of you go to the saloon and hold it up. We'll join you there when we've set fire to the grain store and Jamie has the bank keys. Then the fun can start. Another fire lit in the saloon will give them two blazes to fight. The whole town will be too occupied with that to think of us goin' round the back of the bank and quietly openin' the safe. We could be out of town before they know what's really happened.'

'Sounds fine, Pat,' Jamie said, 'but what about the marshal? He might have something to say about it.'

Their leader laughed harshly. 'He ain't worth a dead gopher. When we raided the Kendrew place them few years back, he stayed in town even after they sent for help. He had a bad back, we was told at my trial. It was the county sheriff who had to do all the runnin' around catchin' us. I don't figure on any trouble from that fat jackrabbit.'

He pointed down to a small group of trees near the stream.

'We'll settle there until dark, have ourselves a meal, and rest the horses,' he said. 'Now let's move.'

Things were not quite as Pat Bullen imagined them in Vane City. As soon as the mayor heard that he had escaped from prison, he suggested that the Kendrew brothers should leave town. They had been quick to take the advice and their store was being tended by hired help. Mayor Vane had also appointed five more deputy marshals and warned them to be ready for a call-out at any time. They were reluctant heroes, and two of them were aiming to leave town as soon as any alarm was raised. Marshal Harlow felt the same way. He started to limp, and had made sure that the locks and shutters on the jailhouse were in good order.

It was young Will Vane who showed a determination that made the mayor feel a little safer. The young man kept his guns loaded and ready. He slept lightly and there was a new spring to his step.

For the first time in his life he had some responsibility other than unpacking dry goods and mopping floors. He wore the deputy's badge with quiet pride.

Another telegraph message from the county seat was reassuring. The escaped man and his rescuers had moved north. They were last seen heading towards Fort Grant and the mountains where they would be able to hide more easily. The county sheriff had a large posse moving in that direction and the military were putting out extra patrols. The mayor breathed a sigh of relief at the news. And so did the marshal.

Thursday evening in Vane City was a quiet time. The main street was in darkness before midnight, and the only lights came from the windows of the saloon where no more than a couple of dozen drinkers were having a final few beers before going to their homes.

The marshal was asleep, and the animals dozing at the Golden Horse hitching rail were undisturbed by the occasional howling of a hungry coyote somewhere on the edge of town.

The mayor sat with his wife over at their store. He was checking over the goods that he had recovered from the wagon of the late J. Samuel Davis. It was a good haul. Books, magazines, rolls of cloth, some hardware items, and a whole plethora of fancy gewgaws for the ladies. He stood to make himself a tidy profit from it all. Then there was the sale of the horses and wagon, and the value of the dead man's guns. It did the mayor's heart good to look at the long list that sat on his knee. He had let cousin Nathan make a little profit on the affair, but not too much. And he had put a small amount into the town funds after making a false inventory of the loot. The rest was his.

The slight glow beyond his window did not penetrate the mayor's concentration, and it was his wife who got up from her chair and crossed to raise the yellow net curtains. She pointed out the brightness over the main street, somewhere behind the corrals that adjoined Adam Smith's market. She called Tobias and he peered through the steamed-up glass, his heart sinking when he realized that Kendrew's feed store was on fire.

He ran quickly downstairs and out of the door of his own store, putting on his jacket as he sped towards the only place in town where men might be gathered in large enough numbers to fight the flames. Others had already beaten him to it and folk were rushing back and forth with buckets of water from the various pumps and troughs.

Nobody came out of the saloon but he took it for granted that they were the ones already engaged in fire-fighting. Others arrived to join the mayor as he ran for the site of the blaze.

The grain store was well alight as the men used their buckets to try and quell the flames. They hurried back and forth from the pumps as shadows danced on other buildings and sparks began to fly in the light breeze.

Somebody remembered to let the horses out from the nearby corrals and the animals went clattering along the street to escape the noise and confusion. Nobody took any notice of the two men who simply walked across the main street and entered the saloon.

Mike and Pat Bullen blinked in the brightness of the long, smoky bar room. Everybody was standing up, most of them with their hands in the air as the rest of the Bullen gang kept them covered.

Mike pulled his own gun and went over to the counter where he picked up an unused glass of beer and swallowed the contents with lip-smacking satisfaction. His brother surveyed the room.

'Where are the Kendrew brothers?' Pat Bullen asked in a loud voice. Nobody answered and he advanced to the counter and cocked his Colt .44 in the face of the bartender.

'I'm askin' just once,' he said, 'and don't tell me they're at the grain store, 'cos they ain't.'

The man gulped as the gun barrel pushed into his flabby neck. 'They left town two weeks past,' he said as he fought for breath. 'The mayor told them to.'

'Then let's just wait here quiet-like,' Pat told the drinkers as he stared round at them. 'Any noise and I'll get kinda put out and start shootin'. I got no quarrels with any of you folk. Just with the Kendrews.'

Almost as he spoke, the swing doors flew open and Jamie Bullen entered. He was grinning broadly and held something in his clenched fist that he waved triumphantly at his brothers.

'I got 'em!' he crowed, and would have said more had not Pat made an angry gesture to shut him up.

'We're leavin' town now,' he told the frightened audience, 'and don't nobody try followin' us.'

He looked round once more, picked up a glass from the bar counter, and flung it at one of the oil lamps that hung from the ceiling. The lamp rocked on its hook and the flames flickered violently for a moment. Pat Bullen cursed and reached up to pull the thing down. He grabbed the copper bowl to wrench it from its moorings and tossed it across the floor, spilling oil and flame over the sawdusted planks. The men all scrambled to the rear of the room while Mike, taking the cue from his brother, took one of the wall lights from its ledge and threw it across the counter to land among the whiskey bottles. Flames shot up the wall as the two bartenders dived for cover to escape the blaze.

The three brothers led their followers out of the saloon while the locals desperately tried to fight the fire that was rapidly getting out of control. The gang walked quietly down the street, unheeded by folk who were more concerned with the trouble at the grain store. The noise inside the saloon now started attracting attention and more lights went on in the windows of folk who were wakened by the noise and the dancing shadows. A few men walking round to the rear of the bank was nothing worth noting.

It was quiet behind the bank. The gang had already tethered their horses there and Jamie had the keys for the building in his sweating hand. He triumphantly opened the rear door to admit his colleagues. They lit a small oil-lamp that was on the banker's desk and took it through to where the large green safe lay ready for looting. The key fitted without any trouble and the door swung back to disclose the contents.

Will Vane had heard nothing of the excitement until the glow of the fires penetrated the lodgings of the schoolma'am. He was courting her, ardently and secretly, in the comfort of her own quarters behind the schoolroom. His uncle would have disapproved. Will was his slave, employed for little more than board and keep as the poor member of the founding family.

The idea that he might strike out independently was something the mayor would not have countenanced. Will, for all his apparent quietness, was shrewd enough to know how things were, and so he kept the luscious Nina Evans his little secret.

He jumped to his feet and, after glancing through the window, strapped on his gunbelt and left the startled woman wondering what had happened.

The town was getting noisy now and the young man ran to the main street where he could see two buildings alight. He then dashed across to the bank, but nothing could be seen through the shuttered front windows. He ran quickly round to the back to find a dozen horses tethered to the porch uprights.

Taking in what was happening, he rushed back to the main street, grabbed the three nearest men and told them to take positions on the boardwalk opposite the bank's front door and to shoot anybody who tried coming out. The startled men did as they were told and watched him a little uneasily as he seized three more of the firefighters and took them with him round to the rear of the building.

He directed the removal of the horses, and then the little group waited in the shadow of the other buildings for someone to come out of the bank.

EIGHT

Nathan Harlow lay on his back, belly gently heaving as he snored through unshaven lips that wobbled petulantly. His scanty hair was unkempt and his podgy hands held on to the bedclothes as if trying to pull them further up his sweaty body. He did not hear the shots that were disturbing the town or see the glow in his bedroom window as the grain store and saloon burned merrily despite all the efforts of the townsfolk.

The marshal slept in a happy, drunken sleep that was undisturbed by anything, even the snores of the fat woman who was at his side. Her long hair lay across the grubby pillow and one bare leg hung off the edge of the narrow bed.

Somebody was hammering at the outer door of the jailhouse and the lawman stirred uneasily as the sounds penetrated to the back room where he lay. He shifted his position and opened one eye lazily. He could hear shouts and more banging on the woodwork of his office. Nathan sat up in bed, reaching out to turn up the wick in the oil-lamp that sat on a rickety bamboo side table. The warm glow made the room a little more homely but showed up the untidy mess of discarded clothing that lay around.

He struggled to his feet, his long combinations stretched to their limits across his stout body, and the thick wool socks half off his unwashed feet.

'I'm coming!' he shouted hoarsely as he kicked the whiskey bottle under the bed. 'There's no call to go knockin' the door down! I'm comin' as soon as I gets my pants on, so just hold the noise!'

He scrambled into some clothing before hurrying through to the front door of his office to open it a little fearfully. The glow of the fire hit him like a sobering jet of water. He suddenly became aware of the shouting interspersed by gunshots as he tugged at his leather braces while admitting the caller.

It was his cousin, the mayor, and Tobias Vane's face was a reddish mask of excitement with sweat trickling down his chin. His grey hair fluttered in the breeze as he pushed into the office.

'Pat Bullen and his gang are in town,' he gasped. 'They've burned the grain store and the saloon, and now they're tryin' to rob the bank. You gotta come and lend a hand, Nathan. We got ourselves some real trouble.'

Marshal Harlow swallowed hastily. 'You turned them deputies out?' he asked anxiously as he reached for his gunbelt in the drawer of the desk.

'Young Will's takin' charge till you get there. The gang's in the bank but he's got both doors covered and as soon as they show themselves the folks will open fire. That lad's got a good head on his shoulders.'

Nathan was loading a shotgun with trembling hands. 'How many of them are there?' he asked.

'About a dozen, I reckon, and we can't spare many men. The wind's gettin' up and could blow the flames on to the other buildings, so fightin' the fire is real important. My store could catch alight at any minute. I could be ruined.'

The marshal laid the loaded shotgun on the desk and now started working on his old Winchester. He shoved the cartridges in slowly as though hoping that everything would be finished before he was ready to step on to the street. Bullets spilled out of the cardboard box as his unsteady hands fumbled among them.

'Has Pat Bullen got his brothers with him?' he asked.

'How the hell do I know?' the mayor snapped impatiently. 'Get yourself out there and let's have this lot behind bars before they do any more damage.'

'What about the telegraph?' the marshal asked desperately.

'The line's down. Now, get out there, Nathan, and settle with these Bullens once and for all. Show them that we got us some real law in Vane City.'

The marshal squared his shoulders. 'You leave it to me, Tobias,' he said grandly. 'Get yo'self safely back to the store and make sure it don't take fire. I'll gather up some more guns and ammunition for my deputies and make sure that they all know what they're doing. I'll have them Bullens in this jailhouse before they know what's hit 'em. If they've killed anybody in my town, it won't be a few years in the territorial jail this time. We'll see 'em hang right here in Vane City.'

He ushered his cousin through the door and carefully locked it after him. Once the mayor was out of the way, Nathan Harlow hurried back to the room where the woman was still snoring drunkenly. He was sober now, and feeling icily cold despite the warmth of the night. He reached under the mattress, retrieved his money-poke, grabbed the rest of his clothes and some food, and went quietly out of the back door to collect his saddle from the lean-to shed.

His horse woke at the noise of the corral gate opening and came over to nuzzle the man who clumsily tried to cope with a rifle, shotgun, harness, and the rolled blankets, all at the same time. He managed to saddle the startled animal before leaping on its back with surprising agility.

71

With a sharp dig of his heels, he spurred it out of the corral, across the side lanes and away from town to the north. Marshal Harlow was leaving Vane City for a wider, safer world.

He was not a hero, and the thought of tangling with the vengeful Bullens had haunted him since he heard that Pat might be broken out of prison. Nathan had enjoyed the prestige of a lawman's badge for seventeen years. He had bluffed his way through life and his poke held plenty of cash for a new career in a quieter place. He had helped the mayor to fleece the town of their birth by every moneymaking trick that could be pulled. Crooked gambling in the saloon, short measure in the stores, and all the bribes for turning a blind eye and a deaf ear to petty crime. All these had enriched the two cousins. Nathan would miss the easy pickings, but he had no wish to be shot by bank robbers.

He rode due north through the darkness with no particular goal in mind so long as it was well away from folk with guns.

The moon was going down and the trail was difficult to follow. The marshal could only move at a cautious pace over the uneven ground. The noises of the night were loud in his ears as he tried to put as much distance between himself and Vane City as possible. He would camp before dawn, have something to eat, and decide on future plans.

He was beginning to feel thirsty after an hour or so. The whiskey was having its effect now that fear was wearing off, and Nathan Harlow had forgotten to bring water with him. He was not quite sure where the nearest stream was located and licked his dry lips as he bounced uncomfortably in the old saddle.

It was as he approached a rise in the ground that he smelled something. It was coffee. Fresh coffee.

He reined in his mount and sat listening carefully for any unusual noise around him. The smell was quite strong, drifting on the wind and teasing him as he listened for some sign of human activity.

Then he saw the glow just over to the west. It was a pale light beyond a clump of tall mesquite and he could make out the flicker of a camp-fire as the bushes stood silhouetted against the night sky.

The marshal bit his lip nervously. Thirst and hunger had vanished now and he was frightened again. Somebody was camping out there and he recalled the area as it looked in daylight. There was a small stream coming from higher ground. It was a natural stopping-place for travellers. He sat for a while, debating on what to do next. Sweat was pouring down his face and dripping on the old leather waistcoat. He at last made up his mind and dismounted, tying his horse to a stunted bush.

He took off his spurs and moved forward slowly in the darkness. He could hear the movement of horses as he got nearer to the camp-fire, and as he peered carefully around the clump of mesquite, he could see the sleeping men.

It was an army patrol of some twenty troopers, settled for the night and with only one man on guard by a fire that was topped by the boiling coffee-pot.

The marshal heaved a sigh of relief as he stood in the shadows, wondering what to do next. He glanced back towards Vane City and, after a long pause for thought, walked boldly into the army camp.

Vane City was in turmoil. The main street was brightly lit by the flames of the burning buildings and sparks were flying around like fireflies on the night air. Will Vane had placed his men well. They crouched behind barrels or water-troughs, keeping the doors of the bank well covered. The front entrance was easily seen in the firelight, and round at the back, Will had thrown some straw and tarred rope within a few feet of the door and set it alight.

The men in the bank were well and truly cornered and their situation was getting desperate.

Pat Bullen had smashed one of the windows to shoot through a small gap in the wooden shutter. He was at the rear of the building and had seen that their horses had vanished. He cursed as he aimed at the uncertain targets beyond the little fire that burned outside the back door.

The money lay at his feet. Four white canvas bags with all the wealth of the bank in notes and silver. And none of it was of any use to him unless he could escape. He cursed again. Not at his own stupidity but at the world in general. Mike and Jamie joined him at the rear windows. They looked worried, their dark faces lined deeply by the sharp, moving shadows from the porch.

'What are we goin' to do, Pat?' Jamie whispered fearfully.

'Make a rush for it.' His brother's voice was tense.

'They've taken our horses.'

'I can see that, but we ain't got a choice.'

Mike saw a figure moving near the corral and took a shot. The flash of the gun lit up the room for a moment.

'You got us into this, Pat,' he said tersely. 'What ideas do you have now?'

Pat Bullen glanced at his brothers before looking round the darkened room.

'Are all the others watchin' the front?' he asked quietly.

'Yeah, why?'

'We close that door back there and push this desk against it,' Pat said with sudden inspiration. 'But only after we've set fire to their part of the bank. There's papers and that carpet that'll burn right well.'

'But they'll all be killed!' Mike protested.

'Of course they won't. They can open the front door and give themselves up, or they can make a dash for it. While everything's happenin' at the front, we'll leave quiet-like through the back door. It'll give us a better chance and we still got the money right here.'

Mike and Jamie looked uncertainly at each other.

'Do you think we can make it, Pat?' Jamie asked dubiously.

'We can try. If them townsfolk think we're all makin' a break out front, they might well pull away some or all of the guns back here. It's the best chance we have. Are you with me?'

Mike nodded reluctantly. 'We ain't got a lotta choice,' he murmured.

'Right. Then no more shootin' back here. We want them to think we're all at the front. Now, let's get that fire started.'

The three brothers moved quietly in the darkened room, gathering any sheets of paper and piling them in the little passageway that led from the rear office to the front of the bank. They found two wicker baskets and a large broom to add to the heap of rubbish that filled the width of the little corridor, and Pat added the contents of an oil-lamp to the collection.

The shooting was furious at the front of the building and the rest of the gang were too busily engaged to see what was happening behind them. Pat struck a Vesta and lit the pile. It flared up instantly and he and his two brothers withdrew to the rear office to push the heavy roll-top desk across the door.

Mike and Jamie went to the window to peer out carefully at the three townsmen who covered the rear of the bank. They were all well hidden, watching from cover for any movement from the building. It was quiet out there and the brothers waited for something to happen.

It soon did. The rest of the gang suddenly realized that the fire was blazing behind them and creeping along the short passage to where they crouched in the main part of the bank. There were shouts of alarm and attempts to put out the flames. It was already too late. The paint on the walls was blistering and the heat drove them back. An oil-lamp burst to fling a brilliant fountain of flame across the bank counter. Some papers and ledgers caught fire as the frightened men cowered near the front door.

The townsmen outside could see the leaping flames between gaps in the shutters, and Will Vane ordered the men to watch carefully in case the gang were planning a breakout.

A breakout never came. One of the gang waved a

hand through the partly opened door and threw out his guns as a sign of surrender. Will shouted for him to come out with his hands high, and all the watchers breathed a sigh of relief when he did so. The others followed. Eight in all. One had been killed and the three Bullen brothers were not among the men surrendering.

It was not possible to know in the uncertain light and all the confusion of the night whether or not the leaders were missing. The gang themselves did not realize at first that the Bullens were not with them. Everything had happened so quickly that they stood looking hopelessly defeated as Will Vane rounded them up into a tight group after making sure that nobody was still armed. They were marched off triumphantly to the jailhouse while word went around that all the trouble was over. Even the fire in the bank was accepted as having been caused by sparks from the other blazes.

Pat Bullen had guessed right. As soon as the town believed that the gang had surrendered, the men guarding the rear of the bank withdrew from their places to join the rest of the town in fighting the fires and celebrating their bravery against a really tough gang.

That was the time that the brothers emerged from the rear door of the bank with the four sacks of money in their grasp. They were fearful at first, and then realized that things had worked out perfectly. Pat led the others across the alley to a small outhouse where kindling and logs were piled untidily amid a carpet of chippings that smelled sweet despite the raw stink of fire doused by water that now pervaded the town.

'What do we do next?' Mike asked fearfully.

Pat peered at him in the darkness of the little shed.

'We hide these bags here,' he said, 'and then we take a walk round all those side lanes and try to find some saddled horses. Just move casual-like. There are so many people around fighting the fires that nobody's goin' to heed us if we just act like normal folk. We get ourselves three horses, come back here, pick up the money, and ride outa town before daylight.'

Jamie looked longingly at the bags of cash. 'Can't we take them with us, Pat?' he pleaded.

'Oh, sure, and have the first fella we see shoutin' that we're carrying' the bank's money all around town. Just hide them back of this timber and let's get outa here.'

His brothers did as they were told and the three men left the small shed to scour the side lanes of Vane City for horses that would help them escape. The town was still in an uproar with people running wildly about trying to stop the flames spreading from roof to roof. Nobody took notice of three men emerging from a corral, each leading a cow pony. There were plenty of animals around. Some were tethered outside buildings while others ran loose after being freed from corrals too near to the burning structures. It had taken the Bullens less than ten minutes to provide themselves with mounts. They walked their animals quietly back to the little shed at the rear of the bank and tethered them to a rail while they entered the shed again to recover the white canvas bags from among the firewood.

Mike and Jamie emerged first. They carried three bags between them which they placed on the ground as they unhitched the horses and prepared to mount. Jamie heard or sensed something happening behind him. He glanced round hurriedly and saw Will Vane standing there.

NINE

Mike was in the act of picking up two of the bags when Jamie let out a yell and went for his gun. He followed his brother's lead, drew his own Colt and let go one wild shot before making a run for it. He left Jamie, the money, and the horses as he dodged round the corner of the shed and tried to vanish into the darkness between the wooden houses.

Jamie Bullen stood his ground. He drew on the deputy marshal as the young lawman unholstered his .44. Jamie was either a good shot or just lucky. As Will Vane cocked the pistol, a bullet took him in the left bicep and swung him round. He went down on one knee as Jamie scrambled aboard his cow pony and fled the scene.

He careered round the corner – spurring the animal so hard that it brushed the wooden wall of one of the houses and nearly unseated him. A quick glance to the rear showed that nobody was in pursuit. He headed straight for the edge of town, where he could vanish in the darkness of the night. Will Vane was left kneeling on the ground, trying to stem the blood that flowed down his arm.

It was a couple of minutes before anybody came to his aid. The mayor arrived with a shotgun in his hands and his coat flying wide as he panted for breath. He recoiled when he saw Will's condition and was also surprised to see that his nephew was alone.

'You all right, boy?' he asked anxiously.

'I just need my arm tyin' up, Uncle Tobias. I'm losin' a lotta blood.'

'I'll get the doctor,' the mayor said as he looked nervously around. 'I thought you had other fellas with you.'

'They should have followed me but I reckon they'll be fightin' the fires. How're things goin' back there?'

'Harry Turner's place has caught alight and there's sparks blowin' all over town. I see'd you runnin' round here and thought as how you'd have other fellas with you. Who did the shooting?'

'One of the Bullens, I think. When we got the others to the jailhouse, two of the townsfolk told me that there were more of the gang than we'd caught. I reckoned that some had stayed back in the bank and might be tryin' to get out the back way. I'd had it guarded but the fellas must have thought that things was all over and gone off.'

The young man glanced at his damaged arm as he scrambled to his feet.

'I'm bleedin' bad, Uncle Tobias,' he said tersely. 'I reckon I'd better get to the doctor's place.'

'Can you walk all right?'

'Yeah, I can make it.'

Will glanced at the three bags of money lying by the two remaining horses. 'Those have to be taken care of,' he muttered faintly.

'Leave 'em to me, lad. You go get that arm seen to. You've done all you can and we've got most of them behind bars. It's all over now.'

Will Vane picked up his fallen gun, stuffed it back in the holster, and began heading for the corner of the lane. He turned as a sudden thought struck him.

'Where in hell's the marshal?' he asked.

'A good question, son.' The mayor laughed harshly. 'He seems to have skipped town. I reckon as how he's halfway to Tombstone by now. You'll be doin' the marshal's job tomorrow.'

Will Vane shook his head either in puzzlement or to clear it. He vanished from sight and the mayor picked up the three white bags and weighed them in his podgy hands. Two were stuffed with paper money and the other was full of silver dollars that rattled happily in the mayor's eager grasp. He looked carefully around, held the three bags firmly, and set off round the back lanes for his store.

Nobody had thought of looking in the little shed. Pat Bullen was still there, his gun drawn as he expected to be shot down at any moment. When all went quiet, he looked carefully out to where the remaining horses waited patiently. The town was still noisy and bright with the fires, but the little lane was completely deserted. Pat edged his way out, carrying the remaining bag of money and intending to take one of the horses and make his escape.

He put his foot in the stirrup but then realized that the white bag was too conspicuous. If he was spotted with it, everything would be lost. He hesitated for a moment before going back into the shed.

A small window let in a little light from the burning buildings as he opened the bag, removed some of the banknotes and stuffed them into his shirt. He then tied the string at the neck of the little sack and hid it carefully under some sawn timber. After a careful check through a crack in the door, he went back to the horses and mounted one of them.

Nobody saw him gallop out of town as he headed away for safety towards the Mexican frontier.

TEN

Marshal Nathan Harlow rode proudly through the darkness, safely surrounded by an army patrol whose help he had bravely enlisted. He told the captain a story that dealt modestly with his own courage and concern for the folk of Vane City.

According to Marshal Harlow, he had been at the centre of things when trouble erupted. With the aid of his young but inexperienced deputy, he had cornered the raiders in the town and a brutal gunfight had broken out. A fire started, and while the deputy held the raiders at bay with the help of some of the townsfolk, the marshal went for military support.

The patrol captain had given him an odd look at that part of the story and exchanged glances with his sergeant. Nathan explained hurriedly that a drunk had wandered into town at that particular moment and told the marshal that he had passed an army patrol on his way in. Nathan had set out to get their aid, knowing that his authority would be greater than that of any other messenger from Vane City.

Captain and sergeant were still in doubt but they hastily saddled up and accompanied the gallant lawman to save the town.

The stars were now bright in a cloudless sky as they galloped off towards the glow in the sky that marked Vane City. They could see the fires as the column topped a ridge to descend the last couple of miles to their destination.

It was there, sharply etched against the colour of the flames, that they saw a lone rider galloping furiously towards the south. The captain signalled with his right arm and three of the troopers broke away to intercept him. The man had seen the patrol and veered off, digging his spurs into the panting animal as he tried to outdistance his pursuers. The rest of the cavalry halted as the three men gradually caught up with the fleeing rider. Their heavier mounts were fresher while the small cow pony was tiring on the heavy ground. The gap closed rapidly.

The hunted man turned in the saddle to fire a shot that echoed across the valley. It silenced the creatures of the night for a moment and only the sound of the galloping horses wafted back to the watching patrol.

Then the fleeing pony stumbled on the uneven ground. It went down on its front legs, recovering slightly as the rider savagely tugged at the reins. The Colt dropped from his hand as he tried to regain control, but the animal was now limping and the three cavalrymen closed in on either side of him. He pulled the horse to a halt and there was a burst of cheering from the ranks as the man raised both hands in a gesture of surrender.

He was escorted back to the column and Marshal Harlow pushed forward to see who it was. He recognized the man from old Wanted posters. They had captured Pat Bullen.

'I know this fella,' Nathan declared proudly. 'He's the escaped convict who led the gang that raided Vane City. His name's Pat Bullen.'

The captain looked down at the captive man who stood between the still mounted soldiers.

'Is that true?' he asked quietly.

'Not a word of it,' the man answered firmly. 'I was just passin' through to Nogales and saw the fire over there. As I turned away in case I got caught up in somethin', these three fellas jumped me. I could see the rest of you back here lookin' mighty dangerous. I didn't know you was soldier-boys. There ain't enough light for that.'

'He's lying,' the marshal snapped. 'He's one of the Bullens. His picture's on the Wanted posters. They're offerin' five hundred dollars reward.'

'Search him!'

It was the sergeant who spoke and his voice was the hard tone of a man instantly obeyed. The troopers got down off their mounts and did as they were told. A large bundle of banknotes was soon emptied out of the man's shirt. He pulled a face and made no more protests when they put him back on his limping horse and started off again towards Vane City.

Matters were now under control in the town. Will Vane's arm had been treated by the doctor and the young deputy had organized things so that enough men concentrated on each fire. Long lines of buckets were being passed smoothly along the streets to where the water was needed. The mayor fussed around, letting everybody see him and giving out shouts of encouragement without actually doing anything himself. The banker was outside his smouldering building, nursing a sore head but more worried about all his missing money.

The town stank of the burnt and wet timbers while sparks and soot still floated in the air to settle on the faces of the workers.

Nobody took any notice of Ma Edgerton as she walked sturdily up the main street to the jailhouse to crowd in with the other women and children who were gazing at the captured bandits and safely insulting them with threats of a hanging while the glowering men hung on to the bars of their cells.

The building was not meant to house so many prisoners. Behind the marshal's office was a short corridor with two cells on either side. The eight men had been divided between three of them. The fourth cell was used for storing all the rubbish that had accumulated over the years.

The only light was a central oil-lamp hanging from the ceiling of the corridor. It was smoking slightly and adding to the smells that filled the small space.

Ma Edgerton pushed through the crowd, made the ritual gestures of hatred, and cast her narrowed eyes on the rusty bars, the bare walls, and the broken glass in the barred windows. Something could be passed through those windows, and that was all she needed to know.

She gave a slight smile and pushed her way back into the main office. The gun rack still bore a few weapons and two boxes of shotgun ammunition, while the cell keys lay in full sight on the marshal's desk. Ma Edgerton's smile grew a little wider as she left the building with the keys in her pocket.

A newly appointed deputy sat in a chair on the porch. He held a shotgun across his knees and gently chewed tobacco while he watched all the other men of the town fighting the fires.

'You got yo'self a good job there, Bill MacDonald,' Ma Edgerton said dryly.

He grinned and spat across the hitching rail.

'Sure beats runnin' around with buckets of water,' he cheerfully agreed. 'I reckon we'll be havin' us a few hangings shortly, Ma.'

She snorted. 'Maybe. But not if you let all them folk fill up the jailhouse. Some smart fella could pass them a gun or two. I reckon as how you need to empty all them folks out before the marshal turns up.'

The deputy looked at her for a moment as the words sunk in.

'You may be right there, Ma,' he conceded uneasily. 'Marshal Harlow don't seem to be around, but I reckon young Will Vane would sure be put out if they escaped.'

He rose from the chair, and as Ma Edgerton walked off, she heard him lumbering across the creaking boards to enter the jailhouse.

A quarter of an hour later she was moving quietly between the corrals at the rear of the building, until she stood beneath the barred windows of the cells. Her darkly dressed figure was barely visible as she tugged a small wooden feed-trough into position and upended it so that she could reach the vague light of the window.

After a struggle with her heavy skirts, she managed to get both booted feet on the upper edge of the trough and peer into one of the cells. She tapped softly on the broken glass until a prisoner came across and stood on a bunk to meet her eye to eye.

'We ain't comin' out a-courtin' tonight, lady,' he said in a brave attempt at cheerfulness. 'You gotta find yourself some other fellas.'

'Where's Pat Bullen and his brothers?' Ma Edgerton snapped.

The man shrugged. 'They lit out on us,' he complained. 'And if I ever catch up with them, it'll be a killin' job.'

'Then you won't be wantin' any help from me,' he was told sharply.

'And what help could you be?'

'I might have gotten you out of here.'

The fellow's face suddenly disappeared as another man took his place.

'I know that voice,' the newcomer whispered eagerly. 'Florrie Edgerton, by all that's holy!'

'Is that you, Brad Newport?' the woman called back. 'I thought as how they'd hanged you ten years since. Where's my three brothers? The other fella ain't got a good word to say for them.'

'We all got trapped in the bank when a fire broke out. They must have skedaddled out the back but we had to use the front door and face that young deputy and all the townsfolk. I reckon as how I was lucky not to be lynched on the spot. Why in hell didn't you send word to Pat? He was relyin' on you.'

Ma Edgerton muttered an unladylike word.

'That tarnation fool, Walt Carol, came ridin' into town askin' for me all open-like. The marshal followed him to my house and near got me involved. I just had to play along so as not to get caught workin' with him. I gave all the information to that drummer fella, but he ended up dead.'

Brad Newport shook his head in disgust. 'So that's what went wrong,' he muttered. 'We should have kept away from this place, but Pat was dead set about gettin' even with them folks what turned him in. Can you bust us out, Ma?'

She chuckled. 'That's what I'm here for, fella. Is the guard still sittin' out there on the stoop?'

'Last I heard, and the door's closed between the cells and the marshal's office. What you got in mind, Ma? These bars is pretty thick.'

'I ain't sawin' bars at my time of life, Brad. Get your hands round these, and when you see Pat, tell him he owes me.'

She shoved the bunch of keys through the window and jumped down from the wooden trough to scurry back home.

The gang soon opened their cells and after creeping into the marshal's office to collect what guns and ammunition they could find, they left quietly by the back door.

While they were looking for some saddled horses in the corrals behind the main street, the marshal and the cavalry patrol were just about reaching the outskirts of town. There were plenty of horses about for the taking but nobody had been thoughtful enough to leave any saddles or harness where it might be stolen.

There was a great deal of cursing among the men and Brad Newport ordered them to split up so as not to attract attention to themselves.

He and one other went down towards the livery stable where roof fires were still being fought. The barber shop was just opposite and a few cow ponies were tethered there. Brad and his companion casually went across to the animals, tightened the girths on a couple, and quietly mounted.

They rode down the main street and into a quiet lane among wooden-built houses, and there they waited patiently for the others to join them after they had found horses for themselves. Two more of the gang arrived within a couple of minutes, and all but one eventually turned up with various types of mounts.

'Right, let's get the hell out,' Brad Newport said tersely. 'Just ride quiet-like up this lane, and turn west on the edge of town. They'll all be too busy to take notice of us.'

'What about young Billy?' somebody asked. 'He ain't here yet.'

'To hell with Billy,' Brad snapped. 'He's had plenty of time to find a horse. He'll just have to take his chances as best he can. Let's move.'

He led the way up the dark and rutted lane, past rows of houses and barns until a clear view of the range lay ahead. There was an audible sigh of relief as the horses stepped on to grass and the wind blew a fresh, cool smell into their faces. The riders increased their speed and one of them almost let out a yell of triumph as they moved away from the stricken town.

It was at that moment of elation that a troop of cavalry appeared ahead, coming over a dip in the ground and outlined against the lightening sky.

ELEVEN

Brad Newport let out a curse and swung his horse round to gallop back into town where he could lose himself among the buildings. He left the others to fend for themselves, and the whole gang fled in different directions as the cavalry troop bore down on them.

The sudden activity alerted the townsfolk, who turned from fire-fighting to see what was happening off the main street. Will Vane was directing the pulling down of a small storehouse to prevent the fire leaping across from the nearly demolished saloon. His arm hurt badly but nobody else seemed able to organize anything and the whole town appeared to rely on him to give sensible orders.

He heard the noise and ran across to the lane that led out of town towards the north. The soldiers were in clear view and shooting had started as the Bullen gang scattered. One of them rode towards the young deputy, waving a stolen shotgun. Will Vane went for his own pistol and fired a single shot. The man tumbled from his horse and rolled over in the dirt.

Another of the gang emerged from the shadows. He was on foot. It was the one called Billy who had failed to find a saddled horse. He tried now to grab the reins of the animal that had just lost its rider. Will Vane shouted to him to halt but the scared man ran after the horse, reaching out urgently for the trailing reins. The deputy fired again and the man tumbled backwards and lay still.

As the cavalry swept down the street and into the other lanes, two more of the gang were cut down with sabres as they fled. One of them fired a shotgun at the captain but the blast smashed the window of a nearby store and the officer cut the man down before he could cock the hammer of the second barrel.

Nobody noticed just what Marshal Harlow was doing, but he was busy making sure that there was always a soldier-boy between himself and any danger. He waved his Colt in the air and loosed off an occasional shot. He gave a few whoops of encouragement, his horse always under firm control and reined in ready to flee.

The fighting was over in a few short minutes. The bodies of the eight bandits lay scattered round the town, surrounded by the locals who were loud in their praise of the army.

Marshal Harlow was quick to let everybody know that he was the man who had brought help to Vane City. He was slapped on the back and would have been led off for a few drinks had not Will Vane hustled all the men away to their fire-fighting duties.

Dawn was breaking before the town was secure again. The flames had died down but the stench still hovered in a thick miasma that drifted like a veil over the place. The bodies of the dead men had been laid out in a row on the stoop outside the jail-house. Marshal Harlow was anxiously waiting for daylight when he could be photographed with them; in the meantime he contented himself with locking up Pat Bullen. He promised the man that he was sure as hell due for a hanging.

The cavalry troop did not stay long. They had a meal, shook hands with a grateful mayor and his councilmen, and then rode out again just as daylight was breaking over the distant hills. Mayor Vane walked wearily back to his store, accompanied by young Will.

'How's your arm, boy?' he asked in a tired voice.

'Sore as hell,' the young man replied. 'I reckon it's started bleeding again. I'll go see the doc when he opens up for business.'

'You did well last night, lad, but you ain't like to get no credit for it. Cousin Nathan's already grabbin' all the glory he can steal. You and me both know he skedaddled like a scared jackrabbit, but he's coverin' up, and folks think he's some sort of hero.'

Will nodded. 'Well, at least we saved the bank's money,' he said.

The mayor tightened his lips. 'Some of it,' he said carefully. 'I reckon that them other two Bullen brothers must have lit out with a tidy sum.'

'I'd forgotten all about them,' Will admitted. 'What does banker Pemberton say?'

'He reckons as how half the money is still missin'. Sick as a starvin' coyote, he is. Dollar bills mean more to these money-lenders than a noisy tail to a rattler.'

The two men laughed and entered the building to have a light meal and a sleep.

The next few days were spent on cleaning up the town. A new saloon had to be built and funerals arranged for two of the locals who had been killed during the shoot-out at the bank. The dead bandits had been quickly disposed of. Their bodies were interred in a mass grave and the mortician had been ordered to place a wooden notice on it to publish their sins for posterity.

Throughout all this, Marshal Harlow strutted round like a conquering hero.

It was when he returned to the jailhouse after a

particularly convivial outing at the temporary saloon, that Pat Bullen called to him from his cell. The marshal opened the door into the little passage and peered through the bars.

'Stop makin' all that noise, fella,' he snarled. 'I feeds yer, and waters yer, and that's as much as you can expect from anyone in this town. Now, what in hell is you hollerin' about?'

'What's goin' to happen to me?'

Pat Bullen was unwashed, unshaven, and his dark eyes were shadowed in the hollow face. He was a worried man.

'What's goin' to happen to you?' The marshal laughed. 'Fella, you is due one big hangin' party, the whole town's gonna turn out for, and I reckon as how the mayor will make it a public holiday.'

'So what's holdin' things up?'

'We're gonna do it all legal-like. Judge Brennan is on his way from Prescott, and you're gonna have a jury, and all the lawyer-talk that folks like. Then we'll hang you high as high. The town's lookin' forward to it.'

Pat Bullen grinned sourly. 'Well, I'm glad to be an entertainment, Marshal. There's just one little thing you can do for me.'

'What?'

'Tell the mayor I want a word with him.'

The marshal stared at the man for a moment. His brows contracted in puzzlement.

'What the hell would you have to say to the mayor?' he asked suspiciously.

"That's for him and me to discuss. You just go get him.'

'I don't take orders from no jailbird killer!'

'Marshal, your job may depend on it. The mayor will want to talk to me.'

Nathan Harlow looked hard at the man again. He wanted to put a fist through the bars and punch him in the face. But there was something in the seriousness of Pat Bullen's manner. He turned on his heel and went back to the office.

Tobias Vane was worried. Nathan's message was something he did not expect and he stood at the window of his upstairs living-quarters, looking out at the street with fierce concentration. He moved to the other window where he could get a better view of the jailhouse. He could see the marshal at his desk. He was playing patience with a cup of coffee steaming near his right hand. Young Will Vane was down in the store. His job as deputy gave him plenty of time to work for his Uncle Tobias. The mayor made up his mind and finally strode firmly across the street to the jailhouse.

He was standing in front of the cell a few minutes later. Nathan had tried to join him but Pat Bullen made it clear that what he had to say was for the mayor's ears only.

'Well, what possible reason can you have for talkin' to me?' Tobias asked pompously.

'They're gonna hang me,' Pat Bullen said quietly. 'Sure as hell's a hot place.'

'Well, I don't figure on havin' that happen. I got other plans.'

The mayor smiled slightly. 'Is that a fact? And how do you aim to escape?'

It was Pat Bullen's turn to smile. His discoloured teeth showed dimly in the sneering mouth.

'I aim to make me a deal,' he said softly. 'A big money deal.'

Tobias leaned a little closer to the bars.

'Go on,' he said after a glance at the door that separated them from Marshal Harlow's office.

'Well, when my two brothers stepped outa that shack, I was still holed up there. They got caught by that young fella, and they lit out. You came on the scene and saw it all happen. Remember?'

The mayor had gone a little pale and he just nodded dumbly.

'There was four bags full of money,' Pat Bullen went on with quiet confidence. 'The damned fools left three of them there on the ground when they ran out on me. I had the fourth.'

The mayor blinked and began to relax. 'You do interest me,' he said warmly. 'So what are you suggestin' then?'

'I'm suggestin' that I didn't take that bag with

101

me when I left town. I just stuffed a few of the notes in my shirt and they was found by the soldier-boys. I still got the rest of them banknotes hid safe away.'

The mayor's eyes were bright now and he licked his dry lips with a small, pink tongue.

'It's not goin' to be easy,' he said slowly. 'The travellin' judge will be here by next week, and the hangman is bein' contacted by telegraph. If the folks round about don't get a trial and execution, I hate to think what they'll do. It's too risky to let you escape.'

Pat Bullen pressed his face closer to the bars. 'You could still have a hangin' if you played it my way,' he murmured. 'I'm just a plain type of fella. With a growin' beard, I figure to look like most folk of my age and weight.'

The mayor's eyes opened wide in horror. 'Are you suggestin' we hang some other fella?' he barked.

'Now you're catchin' on, Mr Mayor. You got some drunks in town? One of them would do nicely. Bring him into the jailhouse when he causes trouble, feed him liquor so he don't know night from day, and hand him over to the hangman. Folk won't notice if they're kept at a distance. Then you can turn me loose when it's all over.'

Tobias Vane was sweating. He gulped loudly as he thought things over.

'It could work,' he said slowly. 'We got one or two

regulars who come into town on Saturday nights, get skunk-drunk and then try causin' trouble. Nathan locks 'em up until they're sober, and then packs 'em off home. Nobody pays any heed to them. It could work.' He poked his head forward eagerly. 'So where's the money?'

Pat Bullen laughed. 'Not so fast, Mayor. You and me has got to trust each other. You can't work this without your marshal. Can you depend on him?'

Tobias nodded. 'He's kin, and he owes me. The young deputy would be a problem, but we could send him outa town on some fool errand. He's a simple lad and won't cause no trouble.'

His eyes suddenly became wary.

'Why did you send for me?' he asked suspiciously. 'You could have made this deal with the marshal.'

Pat Bullen scratched his unshaven chin and the noise was loud in the confined space.

'I figured you for the boss man,' he said. 'Besides, I also figured you for one almighty thief.'

Tobias bridled angrily. 'How dare you...!'

'Come down off your horse. Suppose I was to ask that banker fella how many bags you gave back to him? Or suppose I mentioned it in court? See what I mean? You and me has just gotta trust each other.'

There was silence for a while and then the mayor grinned.

'You have the right of it there,' he conceded. 'I'll

have a word with the marshal and you keep
growin' that beard. Make it a bit full at the sides
and chew some tobacco to dye it round the mouth.'

The mayor left Pat Bullen a few minutes later
and passed through the heavy door into the
marshal's office. Nathan Harlow was seated at his
desk with the patience cards laid out before him.
He was breathing hard and Tobias had no doubt
that only a short time ago he had been listening
with his ear against the door panels.

'You heard all that, I suppose?' he asked sarcas-
tically.

'Heard what?' The marshal tried to look surprised.

'Well, hear this. You work along of me and that
fella back there, and you'll get five hundred dollars
for your trouble.'

The marshal's flabby mouth fell open. 'Five
hundred!' he gasped. 'For that sort of money,
Tobias, I'd hang the territorial governor for you.'

'That won't be necessary, though you'd be doin'
us all a good turn. Now, let's talk over the details.'

It was past midnight and Marshal Harlow had
been taking a quiet pull on the whiskey bottle that
he kept in his desk. The cards were neglected as he
dozed in the large chair. A single oil-lamp burned
above his head and a few moths fluttered around
it, their wings tapping on the hot glass.

The noise of the opening door was enough to

wake the sleeping man. He started up in his chair and found himself looking into the barrel of a shot-gun. It was held by a short, slim man with a face unshaven and hard-looking. It was Jamie Bullen and he looked as if he meant business.

TWELVE

'Get them keys and open up the cells,' the intruder snarled as he held the gun steadily at the stricken marshal.

Nathan picked up the heavy bunch from the desk top and staggered to his feet. His belly heaved under the sweaty shirt as he edged round the gun rack and tremblingly opened the door of the passage that led to the four cells. He walked ahead of Jamie as they entered the unlit portion of the jailhouse. He was made to light the oil-lamp while the gun covered him unerringly.

Pat Bullen was asleep on the bunk, snoring as he lay flat on his back holding on to a rough blanket that was pulled up to his chest. He had not taken off his boots and they stuck out of the covering with the toes pointing to the ceiling.

Marshal Harlow opened the cell door with a great rattling of keys. The noise woke Pat and he leapt to his feet at the sight of his brother

'I got horses round the back,' Jamie told him as he took the keys from the lawman and pushed him into the cell. 'We can be out of here before anyone knows what's happened.'

'Where's Mike?' Pat asked anxiously.

'Haven't seen him. He had no horse when we left town. I bin hangin' around and watchin' things. It's just you and me, Pat. Let's get the hell out.'

Pat Bullen looked at the marshal through narrowed eyes.

'I aim to take me a lawman before I leave here,' he said with soft menace. 'Give me your Colt, Jamie.'

'Forget it!' his brother shouted. 'We don't want no noise. You got us all into enough mess as it is. Just let's get the hell out.'

He heard a slight move behind him and turned his head towards the door leading to the office. A figure stood there, framed against the light and solidly blocking the way.

It was Will Vane with a shotgun in his right hand. The other arm was still bandaged and painful but the young man held the gun steadily as he supported it against his hip.

'Drop it, Jamie,' he said quietly, 'and then join your brother in the cell.'

Pat cursed and made as if to snatch the shotgun from his brother's uncertain grasp. Jamie was staring straight into the barrels of his opponent's weapon, and he hesitated for one fateful moment. Then he began to swing the gun round, his fingers tightening on the triggers.

The marshal let out a yell and Jamie swung the gun back again in case the lawman was armed. His lack of decision was enough.

Will Vane fired and the charge took Jamie Bullen in the chest. Some of the shot was heard clattering on the bars of the cell and Pat Bullen and the marshal let out screeches of pain as they caught some stray pellets in their faces.

Jamie made no sound. He fell backwards with blood pouring from the massive wound. He lay across the doorway of the open cell with the unused gun lying across his legs. Pat looked down at it and then at the steadily held weapon in Will Vane's hands. The deputy still had another unfired barrel and the hammer was pulled back ready for use. Pat Bullen sat down on the bunk in a gesture of resignation while the agitated marshal tumbled out of the cell and dragged the body away from the opening.

'That was good work, lad,' Nathan said as he locked Pat Bullen up again. 'That fella took me plumb by surprise.'

'Your face is bleedin' some,' Will said cheerfully as he went through to the office to open the tin box of bandages and salve that was kept in the desk.

The place was soon full of visitors. The mayor pushed his way in and looked down at the corpse of Jamie Bullen. Everybody agreed that it was a good night's work. Marshal Harlow could be heard telling anybody who would listen how he had played along with the armed intruder and then diverted his attention when Will Vane appeared on the scene.

The mayor took Will aside. 'Is that how it really happened?' he asked.

'Well, he did let out a yell and Jamie didn't know which way to aim the scattergun.'

Tobias nodded. 'He'll take all the credit,' he said glumly, 'and you'll just have to live with it, boy. How did you know what was goin' on, anyway?'

'I was out walkin', Uncle Tobias. This arm's hurtin' like hell and I couldn't sleep. Thought of goin' round to a friend's house for a bite of supper.'

The mayor's eyebrows rose and he managed a slight grin.

'That friend wouldn't be a schoolma'am by any chance?' he asked.

'You know about me and Miss Nina?'

'I ain't nobody's fool, lad. But don't talk to her about things that concern the town. Follow me?'

'Sure do, Uncle Tobias. Anyways, I see this horse outside the jailhouse, and that was surely strange for so late a time. I goes in and finds Jamie Bullen tryin' to stop Pat from killin' Cousin Nathan.'

'Right lucky he was then,' the mayor chuckled. 'Though killin' Nathan might have been a blessin' for Vane City. We need a real marshal. Not some flabby coward who goes runnin' out when trouble starts.'

The young man grinned. 'Like me?' he asked.

'Sure as hell like you. But we're stuck with Nathan, and the more he goes round playin' the hero, the safer his job.'

The mayor stood behind the counter of his store, chatting to the ladies who were spending money. He was a little surprised when Marshal Harlow walked in late one afternoon and invited himself up to the private quarters for a chat. Tobias Vane poured them both a whiskey and sat opposite his cousin to hear what the lawman had to say.

'I bin thinkin' about this job of mine,' the marshal said slowly. 'It could be time I moved on.'

The mayor tried to hide his pleasure at the prospect of losing his cousin.

'Well, you could be right, Nathan,' he said warmly. 'You've made Vane City a safe place and maybe now is the time to go marshallin' in some bigger town. A county job perhaps.'

Nathan shook his head and held out the glass for another drink.

'No, I've had enough of gunfightin' and peace-keeping,' he said. 'Now that old Wally Pearson's near to dyin', I was thinkin' of standin' for election as a councilman.'

The mayor gaped. 'You? A councilman? But, Nathan...!'

'You see, Tobias, folk round here respect me. They kinda think of me as the saviour of Vane City. I reckon that if I got elected, I could even end up as mayor.'

Tobias Vane blinked his eyes rapidly. 'I wasn't thinkin' of quittin' the job for a few years yet,' he said in a hoarse voice. 'You'll have a long time to wait.'

Nathan leaned forward in the chair with a strange, knowing look on his face.

'You could resign,' he said softly. 'Tell them that you wanted to concentrate on runnin' the store, or maybe your health ain't too good. Any reason will do. Then I'll stand for election and we'll still be keepin' the job in the family.'

Tobias jumped angrily to his feet.

'And why the hell should I quit?' he demanded. 'I do a good job and the folks like me. You've no experience in politics, and the only reason you're a hero in this town is because young Will dealt with all the problems we've had lately.'

'That's true enough,' Nathan admitted, 'but only you and me know that. If I'm mayor, Will can be marshal, and you'll still be a councilman. We'd have this town sewn up between the three of us.'

111

'You're talkin' nonsense, Nathan. I've no intention of quitting. And that's an end to it.'

The marshal stood up as well. He towered over his cousin and their large bellies nearly touched as they glared at each other.

'I didn't want to make mention of it, Tobias,' the lawman said grimly, 'but after talkin' to that banker fella, I've come to certain conclusions.'

'Have you indeed? I'm surprised you know such big words.'

'I know big money when I smell it too. The Bullen gang had the bank cash parcelled up in four little sacks. Three of notes and one of coin. You and me both knows that Pat Bullen had one sack of notes. I got five hundred dollars of that and you took the rest. That left three bags.'

The mayor snorted. 'So you can count.'

'Yeah, I can count. Young Will got hisself shot, and them three bags was seen by him. You took charge of them but only two ever got back to the bank. Folk would be real annoyed if I had to start askin' what happened to the other bag.'

Nathan turned towards the door. He stood for a moment with his hand on the gilded knob, looking round the elegant room. The furniture was highly polished; a new harmonium stood in one corner, below a large mirror. There was a Turkish carpet on the floor and an Eli Terry clock ticked away on the far wall.

'If I were a mayor,' he said wistfully, 'maybe I could afford me a room like this. We'll talk about it some other time, Tobias. When you've calmed down a little and got used to the idea.'

The mayor collapsed in his chair when the door closed behind the lawman. His face was dangerously red and a small pulse beat in the left temple. He hurriedly poured himself another drink and swallowed it at a gulp.

'Oh, Nathan, you ungrateful bastard,' Tobias groaned bitterly, 'I'll make you sorry you ever tried to cross me. You'll have to go, dear cousin. You'll have to go.'

The judge arrived two days later and the trial started in the schoolroom. It would normally have been conducted in the Golden Horse saloon, but that was still being rebuilt. A supply of liquor had been quietly stored under the draped table behind which the judge would preside. The jury had their own source of refreshment that enabled them to enjoy the occasion.

Pat Bullen appeared unmoved by the proceedings. He sat there, unshaven, sallow, and barely showing concern with what was going on. The verdict of guilty and the sentence of death only brought a slightly wolfish grin to his face while the audience applauded with all the enthusiasm they would have shown in a theatre.

113

There was plenty of celebrating in the town that night at the prospect of a hanging. It was to be done in style and a gallows was being built right outside the jailhouse in the middle of the main street. It was to be a modern thing with a trap-door and the work was being supervised by the hangman's assistant who arrived from the territorial capital with a carefully drawn-up plan of the job.

Marshal Harlow fussed around, keeping his prized prisoner secure and discouraging visitors. He had even cracked down on local drunks, and several had spent a few days in the cells before they were turned loose with a cuff around the head to send them on their way. Only one was detained. He was from out of town but was always a nuisance when he came in for a weekend of drinking and fighting. He was still drunk now, almost unaware of his location and giving no trouble as he lay in a stupor on his bunk.

For some strange reason, Pat Bullen started drinking, and because he would shortly hang, the mayor did not begrudge him his liquor. He sat in the cell with a whiskey bottle and cursed anyone who came near him. The fighting spirit was gone and he sank into a state of despair.

The hangman arrived on Thursday morning. He drove a small gig pulled by a bay gelding that trotted as though in some fancy race. The man matched his rig; a dapper little fellow who radiated good living and friendliness. His clothes were dark and neat and his round, cherubic face was neatly shaved except for fuzzy sideburns and a small moustache.

His assistant, a heavily built and taciturn man, showed him the scaffold and got a smile of approval. After booking into the hotel, the hangman went along to the jailhouse where Marshal Harlow treated him with considerable reverence.

'You'll have no trouble with this one,' he said firmly. 'He's bin drunk ever since the judge passed sentence, so I reckon as how he don't know what time of year it is.'

The hangman nodded solemnly. 'Takes some like that,' he said. 'Best to let them drink and go quiet-like. Makes it easier for all of us, I figure.'

The marshal agreed and led the way to the cells. Pat Bullen was lounging sullenly on his bunk, while in the cell opposite, the local drunk was snoring loudly.

'What's his weight?' the hangman asked.

'Weight?' The marshal had never thought about such a thing.

'Yes, weight. It's all part of the law these days. We got this table of measures, and the length of the rope depends on the weight of the body. That way, the neck gets broke, sharp as sharp and we have no complaints.'

The marshal shrugged. 'I never heard tell of any

115

hanged fella complaining,' he said tetchily. 'All this business of trap-doors and weighin' folk is too pantywaist for my taste. The last hangin' we had, the fella was just hoisted up over the loadin' beam of the grain store. Didn't even need no hangman. I did the job myself and earned five dollars.'

'Them days is over, Marshal. It's all strictly by the territory laws now.'

The hangman glanced into the other cell.

'What's this fella in for?' he asked.

'Just drinking, same as always. But he takes too much and then starts fightin' and cussin' somethin' awful. I throw him out as soon as he's sober. Now, that's a case where hangin' would sure be a favour to the community.'

The two men retired to the office for a drink in complete agreement on who should be hanged. Pat Bullen was eventually weighed after the grain merchant's machine had been wheeled over to the jailhouse. The doomed man had to be held in position and seemed totally unaware of what was happening. He was then hustled back to his cell where he slumped into a deep sleep.

People brought their chairs to the hanging, and some of them wore their go-to-meeting clothes. It was really a public holiday and the large tent that was serving as a temporary saloon was doing good business.

As the hour drew near, the crowd gathered round the scaffold until it looked as if the whole town was there. Only the preacher was noticeably absent. Pat Bullen had sent a message to the effect that the last thing he needed was spiritual comfort. The preacher stayed away in a huff, though he did say a public prayer at the end of his morning service.

The mortician stood by with his assistant. His face was as miserable as usual because the fee would be a small one. The town never did pay for a decent funeral.

Young Will Vane was also missing. His Uncle Nathan had sent him to an outlying ranch where they were bothered with rustlers. The mayor and the marshal now stood inside the jailhouse with the hangman and his large assistant. They watched as the crowd gathered while the marshal occasionally consulted his silver pocket-watch.

'I reckon it's about time,' he said quietly. 'I'll bring him out.'

He went through to the cells and emerged a few minutes later half-dragging a nearly comatose prisoner. The man's hands were already tied behind his back and his head sagged on his chest as he moved in short, unco-ordinated jerks.

'He sure is the worse for drink,' the marshal laughed. 'I'll need help to get him on to the scaffold. His legs just ain't workin' no more.'

The prisoner muttered a few indistinct words

and almost grinned at the men in the office. The hangman's assistant stepped forward and helped the marshal get him out in to the street. A roar went up from the crowd. It was like the sound of a hungry animal, but with the hatred added that made the more sensitive souls shiver in their Sunday best.

The man had to be dragged up the steps to the scaffold. His feet trailed behind, banging on each step as he muttered to himself. A white hood was placed over his head and the hangman did his job.

It was all over a moment or two later and the body dangled, half out of sight while the audience sat or stood in silence. Then the spell broke, and while some of the women began to sing a hymn, the rest of the citizens roared their approval of what had happened.

The marshal, the mayor, and a few of their cronies, went back to the jailhouse. They left the doctor and the hangman to deal with matters round the gallows. The mortician was also fussing and nobody paid attention to what was happening elsewhere.

Nathan Harlow went straight through to the cells. He unlocked that which contained the town drunk. The man looked sober now and stood up when the lawman appeared.

'Your horse is saddled round the back,' Nathan said in his loud, official voice, 'and your gun's on the pommel. So get the hell outa my town and do your drinkin' some place else in future.'

The man grinned sheepishly, muttered some apologies, and shuffled out of the rear door. The marshal slammed it shut behind him and went back to join the drinkers round his desk.

Nobody took any notice of Pat Bullen as he rode quietly out of town.

THIRTEEN

The grain store was nearly rebuilt and the hammering filled the town all day long. The Kendrew brothers had returned to Vane City and set up again in a shed where the doctor usually housed his gigs. He had willingly loaned it to them until things got back to normal.

The bank was proudly sporting a new roof, and the saloon, resplendent in new paint, was the first structure to be completed. There had been plenty of volunteers to help resurrect the most important building in town.

Marshal Harlow was still the hero. As the man who had cleared their city of a dangerous bunch of killers, everyone looked upon him with respect verging on worship. He strutted like a peacock with his large stomach thrust before him and wearing new woollen shirts that he had bought from his recently-acquired wealth.

Will Vane got some praise from local people, but he was only the mayor's poor relation and a deputy who acted under orders. He went about his various duties without complaint, working mostly for the mayor in the store and seldom required to assist at the jailhouse.

Vane City had gone back to being a quiet town. The marshal's treatment of troublemakers had impressed the whole territory. Even the Prescott newspapers had made mention of the lawman who had been responsible for the end of the Bullen gang. Nobody was going to make trouble in Marshal Harlow's town.

It was a hot, still afternoon with the faint smell of new timber and hot tar lingering on the heavy air. A slim, well-dressed rider came into town. He was clean-shaven with a pock-marked face and cold eyes that missed nothing as he tied his mount to the rail outside the jailhouse. He looked around confidently before mounting the two wooden steps and entering the marshal's office.

Nathan Harlow was asleep in his chair. The room was stiflingly hot with the windows tightly shut and the stove lit to heat a now boiling coffee-pot. The sound of the opening door woke the lawman and he tried to look as if he had been sitting back engaged in some deep and profound thoughts.

'Welcome to Vane City, stranger,' he greeted the visitor, 'and what can I do to help?'

The man smiled a little through stained teeth and sat uninvited in the bentwood chair opposite the desk.

'I just dropped by to ask about the Kendrews,' he said quietly. 'After all, Marshal, I didn't settle with them last time I called on your little town.'

Marshal Harlow shot forward in his chair. The flabby face was pale as he looked hard at the stranger and realized that a clean shave coupled with neat clothes had made Pat Bullen hardly recognizable.

'What in hell is you doin' here, man?' he shouted. 'Suppose some fella spots you?'

'You didn't, Marshal, and you and me was closer than two fleas on a hound-dog. Besides, I'm dead, and nobody thinks of lookin' for a dead man. I came here to settle with the Kendrews. They're the cause of all my troubles.'

The marshal leaned across the desk and spread his large hands in a gesture of conciliation.

'Look, Pat,' he said tensely, 'you got outa Vane City alive. Leave it rest there. If you start anythin' around here again, the folks won't be fooled a second time. You'll hang as sure as hell, and I'll be lucky if they don't string me up next to you for good measure.'

The man at the other side of the desk grinned broadly. It was a cruel grin.

'They might just do that,' he said cheerfully.

'Especially if I was to start gabbin' about how you and the mayor hanged a poor drunk and let me go through the back door under the noses of half the town. You'd sure never explain that away.'

The marshal swallowed noisily and his right hand moved back towards the gun at his waist. Before he could do anything, Pat Bullen's Colt was pointing at his head.

'That would be one wrong move, Marshal,' the man said grimly. 'How would you explain away my dead body? You can't afford to have folk take too close a look or ask too many questions. And the mayor wouldn't like it. Would he?'

Marshal Harlow's hand settled quietly on the desk top as he tried to display an air of confidence.

'So what do you want?' he asked.

'Tell me about the Kendrews. All about them.'

'Well, they hid out when we was told about you comin' to town. Left a lad to run the feed store while they stayed some place out on the range. When you was hanged, they came back again and their store's bein' rebuilt. Mighty fine job bein' made of it, too.'

'And where are they now?'

The marshal shrugged. 'They got a small shed back of the main street. Just behind the doctor's house. They've left their wives and kids outa town and the two brothers is sleepin' in the shed. Leave 'em alone, Pat. Let's have an end to it now.'

The bandit leaned forward and the marshal could smell his breath.

'It'll end when I kill 'em both,' he said savagely. 'They sent me to the territory jail, and nobody does that to Pat Bullen and gets away with it. Besides, I got other business in your nice little town.'

The marshal's eyes narrowed. 'What other business?' he asked.

'The bank.'

The lawman groaned. 'You must be pure loco, fella,' he said despairingly. 'That bank is like a military fort these days. How many men have you got?'

'There are four of us. Why?'

'You couldn't take it last time with a dozen. You've got no chance with four and the new alarm system.'

Pat Bullen grimaced. 'What sorta system?' he asked nervously.

'Well, the bank is still bein' rebuilt,' the marshal explained, 'and so they've put in a guard. He ain't much with a gun, but then he don't need to be. All he has to do is stay in the office with the locked safe. If anybody tries anything, he just pulls on a bell rope that rings the alarm bell on the roof. The whole town can hear the thing and they'll all be out with guns and a length of rope. You'd best get outa Vane City, fella. You got no future here.'

There was a long silence while Pat Bullen thought over what had been said. The marshal was thinking as well. He was considering his own political future and was the first to break the silence.

'I could put you on to a good thing,' he said slowly, 'but I'd want somethin' out of it.'

'A share?'

'No.'

'What then?'

'Let me put it this way. I got ambitions in this town, and I don't figure on endin' my life just bein' a lawman. Maybe we can help each other.'

Pat Bullen stood up and crossed to the stove. He filled an enamel mug with hot coffee before sitting down again.

'I'll listen,' he said as he took a sip.

'You can't tackle the bank, but you could hold up the wagon from the lumber company. They collect cash from town every month to pay the wages. It's big money and all they do is to send in two men on a supply rig to buy food from the stores. They go round to the back door of the bank, pick up a small cash box, and hide it among the sacks of flour and other stuff. Then they just drive outa town all innocent-like. If you knew when they was arriving, you and your men could be layin' for them. They'd be right easy to take.'

'And what do you get out of it, Marshal?' Pat Bullen asked with a slight sneer.

'I'd want to catch some of the hold-up men,' Nathan said.

The bandit laughed. 'I should hand over some of my folks to you? You sure as hell got a nerve.'

'Think about it, fella. The less men you have, the less you have to share.'

Pat Bullen's eyes flickered. He scratched his chin in thought.

'You could have somethin' there,' he admitted. 'My brother Mike is the only one who matters. The other two are just a couple of roughs he joined up with while he was tryin' to find me again. How do we go about it?'

'I'll give you the date of the collection and you hold up the rig. They have to pass Tarantula Gulch on the way back to the lumber camp. It'd be a good place to grab the money. Then go along the gulch to the small canyon at the southern edge. Kill the two fellas you don't need and leave 'em there with their guns and horses. I'll come along later, pick 'em up, and tote 'em back to town. Capturin' two of them won't do me no harm, and losin' the money ain't my fault. I'll be on my own against a desperate gang.'

Pat Bullen turned it over in his mind and then broke into a mean grin.

'You sure is one crooked lawman,' he conceded with admiration. 'But what about the Kendrews? I ain't lettin' up on them.'

Nathan nodded agreement.

'You can't risk takin' them in town,' he said, 'but they visit their families each Saturday and stay on

126

the range until Monday. I'll find out what route they take and you can deal with 'em out of town. But get the money first. In case anything goes wrong.'

'Marshal, I wish I'd met you sooner,' Pat Bullen said as he stood up to leave. 'Let's shake on it.'

The two men extended their hands and the deal was concluded.

FOURTEEN

The sun was past its peak as the wagon left town. It was a small rig, pulled by a pair of overfattened horses that moved along at a sedate pace while the two men on the sprung seat smoked their pipes serenely. There were barrels behind them; sacks of grain and flour, and wooden boxes of soap, butter, and all the other necessities for a large logging camp.

The dust rose in a pale red cloud behind them, dry to the mouth and hanging in the still, warm air. They had left Vane City well refreshed by several beers and were completely unready for the sudden appearance of four riders who converged on them from the back of a tall stand of trees.

The driver tried to whip up the heavy horses, but they did not respond to the unusual demand. The other man grabbed for the shotgun that lay at his feet, but he was too late. A volley of pistol fire shattered the air and both men stumbled from the rig and rolled across the ground, dead or dying.

The shooting did to the horses what a smack of the reins would not accomplish. They speeded up in fright and Pat Bullen had to chase the rig for several hundred yards before he could grab their harness and gradually bring them to a shuddering halt. The others joined him and scrambled down from their mounts to search for the money.

It was a small tin box, hidden in a sack of apples, just as the marshal had said. Pat tore off the lid to disclose the pile of banknotes and the little paper bags of coin. He looked at his men with a grin before transferring the money to his saddle-bag and leading the way to Tarantula Gulch where the loot would be divided. He gave his brother a silent wink as they turned their mounts away from the rig.

Tarantula Gulch was nothing much more than a narrow gap formed by a dried-up river centuries ago. It was arid, with only a few scattered bushes growing among the rocks and reddish earth. The four bandits rode into the confined space, their progress heralded by echoes from the fissured slopes as they moved.

A fire was lit and a coffee-pot hung over it. They used some of the supplies from the lumber camp rig and sat down to a hot meal. It was a peaceful setting with the men stretched around the coffee-pot and the horses chomping away at the low bushes and bits of grass that lined the gulch.

It was Pat Bullen who made the first move. He rose from the ground, flung the dregs of his coffee into a patch of yellowish lichen, and then made as if to clean out the mug with dry sand. Nobody took any notice as he quietly slipped out his Colt and shot one of the seated men in the back of his head.

Mike Bullen jumped to his feet, drawing his gun as he did so. The remaining bandit struggled to reach his own pistol but the two brothers fired at him before the gun was even out of its holster. He slumped sideways, his right hand falling against the hot coffee-pot and upsetting the contents on to the sand.

'Well, now we've broken up the partnership,' Pat said with a grin. 'I reckon that leaves just you and me, Mike. We'll high-tail it out of here and leave these two for the marshal fella.'

'Can we trust him?' Mike asked dubiously.

'We don't have to. If he ever goes back on us, he'll have to explain why I'm still alive and who hanged some harmless drunk. That marshal is bought and paid for, fella. Believe me, he won't let us down.'

Pat went across to his horse and tightened the girth. His brother did the same. They then collected the remains of the food, packed everything into their saddle-bags, and mounted the patient animals.

Neither of them saw the man who lay behind the pile of fallen rocks and who had a Winchester trained on them. Marshal Harlow was sweating in the heat and his hand trembled as he sighted the rifle at Pat Bullen. He was scared, and he had to take both men before they had time to retaliate or make a dash for the mouth of the gulch. He was beginning to regret his plan, but the moment had come when he had to go through with it.

The shot echoed between the walls of red stone and Pat Bullen slid backwards off his horse to roll on the ground in agony. Mike drew his Colt and looked round in a panic-stricken way. He could not be sure where the shot came from. The echo had made it hard to locate.

He glanced over at his brother and then decided that he must look after himself. He was too conspicuous on a horse and he scrambled down from the saddle to head for cover behind some mesquite. Before he could reach safety, a second shot was fired from a group of rocks just ahead of him. He stumbled as the bullet took him in the left leg. Then he recovered and tried to find shelter. Before he could move another yard, a third shot caught him in the side of the chest and he dropped on the spot.

There was a long silence. Nathan Harlow did not stir from cover until he was sure that both men were dead. Sweat formed narrow rivulets down his dusty cheeks as he watched for signs of life to end. Pat Bullen was still moving slightly, rolling from side to side and groaning. Mike was dead, his pistol near one clenched hand.

Nathan waited until Pat was silent. Then he stood up slowly, the Winchester cocked ready for use again. He advanced towards the bodies and inspected each one carefully. They were all dead and he had the loot from the lumber camp.

It took him half an hour to manoeuvre each body across the saddle of a horse. He tied them on carefully and then made sure that all their guns were gathered from the dust. The small tin box was in his own saddlebag now and he cheerfully led the four horses with their dead burdens out of the gulch.

It was early evening when Marshal Harlow got back to Vane City. The main street had been quiet until the stream of horses arrived with the bodies of the robbers tied across their saddles. The hold-up had already been reported by a ranch hand who had been on his way into town. The mayor had gone to the jailhouse to alert Nathan Harlow but was surprised to discover that his cousin was missing.

He sent young Will out to the scene of the crime and Will had returned with the news that the bandits had left no trail that could be followed. A blustery wind had blown across any possible tracks and the scent was cold.

The arrival of the marshal was a cause for celebration. He handed the bodies over to the mortician, loaded all the guns into the jailhouse, and proudly turned over the recovered money to banker Pemberton.

Nathan was once again a hero, and modestly accepted the praise that poured in from every side.

Only the mayor was annoyed. His cousin was now far too popular to undermine and Tobias was fearing for his own future as leader of the community.

'You did well back there,' he said as the two men sat in the jailhouse later and shared a bottle of whiskey. 'How come you was on the spot, Nathan?'

'Just good luck, I reckon,' the marshal replied smoothly. 'I'd ridden out to see if there was any sign of them cattle that went astray last week. Picked up a trail for a while and then it petered out. The wind was real fierce out there around noon. I was just turnin' for home when I come across these four fellas ridin' hell for leather to the north.'

'And you challenged them?' the mayor asked sceptically.

'Hell, no. I figured on them bein' ranch hands goin' some place. Then one of them must have seen my badge glintin' in the sun, so he takes a shot at me. I knows then that I'm on to some dirty work.'

'So you chased 'em?'

The marshal shook his head modestly. 'Not really,' he admitted. 'I gotta confess to you, Tobias, that I was a mite scared at there bein' four of them. So I stopped my horse and tried a couple of shots with the rifle.'

He grinned sheepishly. 'I must be a better gunslinger than I figured. Two of them comes down off their horses in good style. Then I feels a little better with only two to deal with. So I gets up speed and chase 'em into a little gulch. Tarantula Gulch, they calls it.'

'I know the place,' the mayor said.

'Well, they dismount and get behind some rocks. After that it was just a shootin' match, and I reckon I was better than they was. It was only later that I found the box of money in one of the saddle-bags. So I brings it into town and hands it to the bank.'

'You're a very brave man, Nathan,' the mayor said in a neutral voice.

The marshal poured them both another drink. 'I just did what I figured needed doing,' he said bashfully. 'But that brings up another point we discussed some time ago, Tobias. I ain't gettin' any younger and all this shootin' and gallopin' about is more than I want to be doin' at my age. I feel that I ought to be settlin' down. Now, you got the store and plenty of money put by. I got nothin' if I retire. So, I reckon as havin' a word with the council and standin' against you for bein' mayor of Vane City. Nothin' personal, cousin. Just common sense.'

The mayor tightened his lips angrily but managed to control his temper.

'And you're a man for common sense as we all know, Nathan,' he said softly. 'But you'll have to fight for the job. I ain't goin' to give up easily. Not even to kinfolk.'

The marshal grinned. 'Well, I'm a fightin' sort of man myself,' he said cheerfully.

Before any more could be discussed, Will Vane entered the office and wearily poured himself a cup of coffee. The two older men stopped talking of personal matters as though by some unspoken agreement.

'Have the bodies been identified?' the mayor asked sharply.

'No, not really, Uncle Tobias,' the young man answered. 'But a couple of folk think that one of them is Pat Bullen's missin' brother, Mike.'

The mayor nodded. 'That would make sense,' he muttered. 'He could still have been around here somewhere. Well, if it is him, that finishes the whole Bullen family and we're well rid of them. All the same, a hangin' would have been better, just like we gave his brother. Folk enjoy a good hangin' and it brings them into town to spend a bit of money.'

He rose to go and the glance he threw at the marshal was not a friendly one.

'We'll talk some more, Nathan,' he said as he nodded his farewell. 'You come back to the store with me, Will. There ain't no work for you here. The marshal has cleaned up all the local crime by himself.'

He ushered the young man out of the jailhouse and across the street. Once inside the private rooms, the mayor sat his young companion down and stood in front of him like some prosecuting counsel.

'How did he kill them fellas?' he asked bluntly.

'Shot 'em,' Will replied as if surprised at such a question.

'I know that, damnit, but how? That cousin of mine is one big bladder of rancid fat. He takes on four robbers and brings 'em all back dead. So how did he do it, boy?'

Will thought about it. There was a slight hint of amusement on his calm face as he delayed answering for a while.

'Three was killed with .44 calibre bullets,' he said slowly. 'The doc dug 'em out for me. The fourth man was shot with a .38 and a .44.'

The mayor slapped his hands together in delight. 'I knew there was somethin' wrong with his story,' he crowed. 'Nathan didn't have a .38 Colt. His .44 matches the Winchester. Somebody else was involved. Go on, lad. Anythin' more?'

'Well, one of them was shot at close range

through the back of the head. His hair was all burned up.'

The mayor nodded his satisfaction. 'Well, that certainly don't sound like no shoot-out,' he said with quiet conviction. 'Cousin Nathan has been doin' somethin' he ain't willin' to talk about. Any more?'

Will Vane paused for a moment and then shook his head.

'Good, then let's get back to work. There's a load of flour to be moved into the back room. And when you've done that, you can clean them windows again. That wind's left 'em all clouded over.'

He dismissed the young man and settled down to read the newspapers that had arrived that day from Tombstone. Will left the building, ignoring the bags of flour and the dirty windows. He walked down the street to the mortician's parlour and opened the curtained door to the tinkling of the warning bell.

'I'd like another look at them bodies the marshal brought in,' he told the mortician.

The man looked at him with morbid interest and led the way to the room at the back of the building where the corpses were laid out on tables ready for placing in their coffins.

Will stared down for a long time at one of the bodies before thanking the mortician and leaving. The man was anxious to know what the deputy

137

was thinking, but Will gave nothing away and went off to move bags of flour and clean windows.

FIFTEEN

The simple funerals of the four bandits were well attended by the people of Vane City. It was something of a celebration and the man at the centre of it all was Marshal Nathan Harlow. He revelled in it and was already having quiet talks with various councilmen about the job of mayor.

They were easily convinced. To be seen siding with the local hero would not do them any harm, and each of them believed that the present mayor was getting too greedy and was too difficult to control. Most of them felt that a simple man like the marshal would be easier to dominate and steer along the right paths of municipal corruption.

This was made plain to Tobias at several council meetings, and he returned home from one in a furious temper. Nathan Harlow's name had been put forward by the councilmen to be next mayor. With that sort of support and public backing, Mayor Vane could see his career of graft coming to an end.

After finding fault with everything in the store, he finally told Will what was happening to his civic career. The young man listened silently, surprised to see his uncle virtually in tears as he railed against Cousin Nathan for betraying the very man who had made him marshal.

'What can I do, boy?' the mayor wailed. 'You and me both know that he's a coward. He'd run away from an angry prairie dog and turn tail if a drunk raised a fist to him. You rounded up the Bullen gang and dealt with all the other troubles we've had in town. But that barrel of molasses stole all the credit, and may the Good Lord forgive me, but I let him do it. After all, he is my kin, and no longer a young man. He's betrayed us all.'

Will Vane leaned on the broom he had been using.

'Uncle Nathan is not an honest man,' he said thoughtfully.

The mayor snorted.

'Honest! He's a bigger criminal than most of the men he arrests. I could tell you stories, boy...!'

He stopped and looked a little uncomfortable.

'What would you be suggesting?' he asked suspiciously.

'Well, he could be investigated for some of his activities,' Will said. 'Even if he wasn't brought

before a judge, the fact that the public found out
how he behaved....'

The mayor shook his head violently. 'No, no. That
won't do, lad. When a lawman behaves badly, it
gives the whole council a bad name as well. We
don't want to throw any dirt around. Dirt can rub
off on innocent people. And after all, I'm the mayor,
and his cousin. It could reflect on me. No, I reckon
he has me hog-tied, and no mistake.'

Will Vane was silent for a few minutes while the
mayor absent-mindedly rapped the top of the
counter with nervous fingers.

'There is one possibility,' Will said at last.

'What? What you got in mind, boy?' The mayor's
voice was desperate.

'Bein' mayor of Vane City is quite a good job,'
Will said slowly, 'but I reckon that a man with your
experience of politics could make himself a reputation in a wider way.'

Tobias puckered his eyebrows in puzzlement.

'What are you saying, boy?' he asked sharply.

'Well, there are elections for the territorial legislature soon. You'd have the support of most folks if
you stood as a candidate, and it's one hell of a high
honour.'

Tobias looked hard at the young man's impas-
sive face. He ran a slightly trembling hand across
his chin as he considered the matter.

'You might have the right of it there, lad,' he

murmured. 'A member of the legislature, yes. And we're headin' for statehood in the next few years. Now, that's somethin' to think about, ain't it? I do believe you've hit on the answer to all our problems. You're a good boy, Will, and I'll see you're made marshal before all this is over.'

'You'll do it, Uncle Tobias?'

The mayor's eyes were alight and a slight smile curved the full lips.

'Oh, no, lad. I'm stayin' here in Vane City. Cousin Nathan can go to the legislature. If I suggest it to the council, they'll think no honour is too great for their hero. He'll get the support of the whole town, and he won't be able to refuse it. Not that I think he would. What a solution!'

'I would have thought you'd prefer the honour, Uncle Tobias.'

The mayor laughed heartily. 'Honour's an empty thing, boy,' he chuckled. 'You have to understand how politics works.' He patted the young man's arm. 'I got this town sewn up. Everybody lines my pocket one way or another. That's what bein' mayor is all about. If I was in the legislature, it would all be new, and I'd certainly be worse off as far as cash money was concerned. No, boy. Nathan can have all the honour. I'll recommend him to the council first thing in the morning.'

Tobias Vane did exactly that, and the council was

delighted at a simple solution to their problem. Although they longed to be rid of the present mayor, it could very well be a case of sticking with the devil you know rather than siding with the one you don't. His proposal was accepted almost unanimously, and they all trooped across to the jailhouse to put the idea to Nathan. The marshal was as keen as anybody else to fall in with their plans, and as word got around Vane City, there was no doubt that the whole town was going to support their hero at the forthcoming legislature elections. Nathan Harlow was as good as elected before he had even made a speech.

Will Vane watched everything that was happening with a quiet look of satisfaction on his face. He worked as hard as ever in the store and helped out the marshal when the ranch hands and lumber men came into town to spend their hard-earned money. He just waited patiently for events to take their course.

Things happened soon enough. Marshal Nathan Harlow was elected a member of the territorial legislature. The mayor was confirmed in his job, and young Will Vane was picked as marshal of Vane City.

There was a special little ceremony in the room over his uncle's store where the councilmen held their meetings. He was handed his badge, took an oath to maintain law and order, and everybody present shook his hand. He almost seemed to grow in stature in front of their eyes as he left them to debate other matters and crossed the street to the jailhouse.

Tobias watched him go with an uneasy look on his chubby face. There was something in the young marshal's manner that was vaguely upsetting. His false political cheeriness was gone as he moved to the window to watch the youth cross the street. The mayor quickly excused himself from the group of men and hurried downstairs.

Nathan had not yet moved out. He was due to leave for Prescott at the end of the week, but until then, he still occupied the room behind the office and gave Will a cheerful welcome when the young man arrived.

'I reckon as how you'll make a right good marshal, fella,' Nathan said warmly as he shook hands. 'Just remember all the things I taught you and always watch your back.'

'I'll do that, Uncle Nathan.' Will looked round the office. 'What happened to the horses, guns, and saddles you got from them fellas we buried a few weeks back?'

The ex-marshal looked startled for a moment. Then he grinned and closed one eye in a massive wink.

'Now, that's the sort of thing you gotta learn

about, Will. All them is what you might call a lawman's pickings. Ted Weller buys the horses and saddles, and Pete Walsh buys the guns. And don't you let 'em cheat you when you got somethin' to sell. Make it clear from the start that you don't aim to be an easy mark for every crook in town. And remember, lad. You gotta give my cousin Tobias his cut. He don't let anybody get away with nothing.'

Will put his hand near the stove to see if it was lit. It was, and he placed the coffee-pot on top and looked around for the white bag that contained the makings.

'You never did identify them four fellas, Uncle Nathan,' he said as he spooned in the crushed beans.

The ex-lawman shook his head. 'Never did,' he admitted. 'Some folk were sure that Mike Bullen was one of 'em, but the other three was all unknown. Why'd you ask?'

'I recognized one of them.'

The self-satisfied look vanished from Nathan's face.

'Which one?' he asked fearfully.

'The fella that was all pock-marked.'

Nathan's hand had crept round to the gun at his waist. He had already noticed that the new marshal was not carrying a weapon.

'Have you mentioned it to anyone?' he asked in what he hoped was a casual voice.

145

Will shook his head. 'No,' he said. 'I thought I'd talk it over with you first.'

'Best way, Will. These things are all sort of official. Not for the folk to be told about unless it concerns them.'

'You haven't asked who I thought it was, Uncle Nathan.'

'No, nor have I. I reckoned as how you'd tell me when you was ready, son.'

'It was Pat Bullen.'

Nathan's fat face seemed to collapse and his rheumy eyes were full of terror. If Will had any doubts, they were immediately relieved by his uncle's trembling hand that was now within inches of the butt that lay at his waist.

'You gotta be joshin' me, lad,' the ex-marshal managed to say between quivering lips. 'You was here when we hanged Pat. The whole town saw it happen.'

'Somebody was hanged, sure enough, but I wasn't here. I'd been sent outa town on a false trail. It was all over when I got back and the drunk in the other cell had been sent on his way. Pat Bullen was the drunk. You just changed them over and hanged an innocent man.'

'Now, lookit here, lad. I don't have to take that from a greenhorn kid like you!' the marshal blustered. 'Pat Bullen was hanged fair and square. The whole town knows it.'

'Uncle Nathan, you've got some pock marks on your face. How did you get them?'

The ex-lawman's hand went up automatically to rub his cheek.

'You know full well how I got them,' he said. 'You fired that shotgun and some of the slugs hit me.'

'That's right. And some of them also hit Pat Bullen. He was standin' there next to you and you both got peppered. The face of one of the dead men was marked just like that. It was Pat Bullen. I shot him in the face when I was tryin' to save your life. The doc's had a look at the body and he agrees with me. Pat Bullen was never hanged.'

Nathan Harlow's face was dripping sweat.

'So what is you figurin' on doin' about it, boy?' he asked nervously.

'I'm figurin' on puttin' you behind bars, bringin' in the travellin' judge, and seein' you hang.'

'Like hell you will, boy!'

The ex-marshal's right hand went swiftly down to his side and the Colt leapt from its holster, cocked and pointing at Will Vane.

The single shot was deafening in the small office and threw out a haze of acrid smoke. Will Vane stood with the coffee-pot in his hand, ready to fling the scalding liquid as he had intended. It was half-raised but no longer necessary.

Nathan had reeled back, the gun dropping from his fingers as he clutched the side of his head while letting out a yell of pain and rage. Blood dripped from his damaged ear and he cursed at the man who stood framed in the doorway.

Mayor Vane was still holding a derringer in his hand. He had not cocked the other barrel and seemed unsure about what to do next. He looked almost appealingly at young Will.

'I had to do it, lad,' he said sadly. 'He was goin' to shoot you.'

'You stupid old goat!' Nathan screamed. 'You damned near killed me.'

The mayor put the gun back in his coat pocket and went over to the ex-marshal so that his bulk was between the two men.

'I bin listenin' at the door,' he said quietly. 'You seem to have some questions to answer, Nathan, and shootin' the boy here ain't gonna look good for you. Now, just step into one of them cells and we'll hold a proper enquiry into what's happened. You know you can rely on your kin to do what's best.'

Tobias winked at his cousin as he took the man gently by the arm and led him down the passage to one of the empty cells. He ushered the ex-marshal inside and stood patiently while Will Vane turned the key.

'I need the doctor!' Nathan shouted through the bars.

'I'll send him to you,' the new marshal promised as he and the mayor headed back for the office to face the crowd that had poured through the open door.

It took a while for them all to disperse. The mayor told them of Nathan's misdeeds, shook his head sadly over such failings among his own kin, and then, after opening a bottle of whiskey, he sat down opposite Will Vane.

'When you left the store,' he said as he poured, 'I figured as how you meant trouble for someone. It was written all over your face. I never guessed who, and you'd left your gun at home. I saw you from the window, going into the jailhouse and havin' some right angry sort of talkin' with Nathan. I figured the best thing to do was to grab a gun and come over.'

Will grinned. 'You was just in time, Uncle Tobias,' he said. 'He'd have sure as hell shot me, but a few more inches and you'd have killed him.'

'Oh, I never would have done that, son,' the mayor said piously. 'I just aimed to hurt him a little. I'm a bit out of practice but it wasn't bad shootin' for an old-timer.'

'No, it wasn't. I suppose the next thing I have to do is to telegraph Prescott for a judge.'

'That's the procedure, son.' The mayor shook his head sadly. 'I can't figure Nathan. I knew he was a man rather over-fond of money, but it's hard to believe that he did the things you said he did.'

'Well, the bank didn't get much more than half the money back, so Pat Bullen must have had

149

enough to bribe Uncle Nathan, and then some.'

'I reckon. Well, I doubt we can save him from a hanging. The Bullen gang caused too much trouble for Nathan to find any sympathy in this town.'

Tobias left a short time afterwards and Will went along to the cells to make sure that his prisoner was all right after the doctor's rough and ready treatment of the bullet wound. They talked for a while and then Will Vane took a walk down the main street to have a word with banker Pemberton.

After giving Nathan some supper, Will locked up the jailhouse with extra care and went across to spend the night in his usual lodgings. He had intended to live at the back of the jailhouse, but all Nathan's things were still there and the place needed a good clean to get rid of the musty smell.

'I would have thought you'd stay there the night,' the mayor said huffily. 'He's one important prisoner, is cousin Nathan. If he broke out, you'd be a very sorry man.'

'I couldn't stay there, Uncle Tobias, and you don't have to worry. He ain't goin' no place. I've got the only keys and that jail is shut up tight.'

The mayor shrugged dubiously and the two men sat down to Mrs Vane's large supper.

When the marshal opened up the jailhouse the next morning, the first thing he did was to take

Nathan's breakfast to him. The mayor's wife had prepared it and the food smelled good under the linen cloth that covered the copper tray.,

But Nathan Harlow never ate his breakfast. He was dead.

SIXTEEN

The councilmen sat round a large table in the room above the mayoral store. The air was thick with tobacco smoke and they all had glasses of whiskey in front of them. Their expressions were of serious civic responsibility as they listened to Marshal Will Vane in awed silence. He told them of the way Nathan Harlow had taken money from Pat Bullen in exchange for hanging a drunken man and letting the gang leader go free.

There was a ripple of amazement as he went on to tell how the mayor had saved the lawman's life when Nathan drew a gun and tried to shoot the young marshal. The assembled men hung on his every word, and when the narrative was over, they burst into a chorus of congratulations to their new law-enforcer and to the mayor who had been shrewd enough to appoint him and brave enough to step in at a dangerous moment.

Banker Pemberton heaved a sigh of deep satis-faction. He had suffered more than most from the activities of the Bullen gang and it would still be weeks before his head stopped hurting and his business got back to normal.

'Well, I reckon we're one lucky town to have a marshal like young Will here,' he said proudly. 'Nathan was always a doubtful character and I never did really support him for the territorial legislature. We're better off now he's dead. I think we all agree on that.'

The rest of them agreed hastily and the mayor led the condemnation of the dead man as he poured out more of his best imported whiskey.

'It's as well he killed himself,' he said piously. 'Saves all the expense and ill-feelin' of a public trial. After all, bad as he may have been, he was my kin, and I'd no wish to see him hanged. He took the best way out and it does save us all a lot of unpleas-ant publicity.'

The doctor gave a little cough and looked mean-ingly at Will Vane. Some intangible signal seemed to pass between the two men. The marshal cleared his throat to speak again.

'Tell us how he went about killin' himself, Doc,' the marshal said in a neutral voice.

'Well, now, he seems to have taken off his shirt, tied part of it to one of the bars, and then just fastened the rest of it round his neck. After that, he slumped down and let himself choke to death. His own weight killed him, you might say.'

'Mighty unpleasant way to go,' one of the councilmen said queasily.' It must have taken one hell of a lot of guts.'

The doctor nodded. 'Showed great determination. I've seen it done once or twice before. If you've got the nerve, you don't have to swing in the air to be a suicide. But not a way I'd care to go. Much too uncertain.'

He glanced across at Will again. It was as if the two men were sending messages to one another.

'Any other marks on the body, Doc?' the marshal asked.

'Funny you should mention that,' the medical man said slowly. 'There was a bad graze at the back of the skull. He either cracked it on the bars or somebody hit real hard.'

There was a murmur round the table and the mayor's eyes narrowed angrily.

'But that couldn't be, Doc,' he snapped. 'Young Will assured me that he locked up the jailhouse before comin' over here for the night. Isn't that a fact, Will?'

'That's true,' said the marshal.

'Then Nathan was alone,' the mayor insisted. 'Nobody cold get near him.'

'Unless there was another set of keys,' Banker Pemberton said in a very low voice.

'I've only got one set,' Will Vane said as he produced the bunch from his pocket and laid it on the table.

The druggist, who acted as secretary to the council, looked up from his notebook.

'There was another set made,' he said. 'Many years back. I remember them being paid for out of town funds.'

'Then who had them?' asked the saloon keeper.

They all looked at the mayor. He opened his mouth but no words came out. His face had gone pale and his hands, resting on the table, were visibly twitching.

'I probably have them about the store someplace,' he finally admitted. 'But I've no idea where they'd be. Perhaps someone stole 'em.'

'Perhaps you used 'em last night,' Will Vane said in a suddenly hard voice.

The mayor swallowed. 'That's a terrible thing to say,' he moaned. 'Are you suggestin' that I entered the jailhouse and killed my own cousin?'

Will Vane stood up. 'I'll tell you exactly what you did, Uncle Tobias,' he said quietly. 'You took your set of keys and went across to the jailhouse at one o'clock in the morning. You entered through the back door, told Nathan that you had a horse saddled and ready to go, and when he went to his room to get his money-poke, you hit him on the head. Then you dragged him back to the cell and

155

rigged the hanging. It was as easy as that.'

The mayor struggled to his feet. 'That's a load of mule droppings!' he shouted. 'Nobody's goin; to believe a made-up tale like that. I've got a reputation in this town, and no wet-behind-the-ears kid is goin' to take that reputation away. I made you, lad, and I can just as easily break you. Don't forget that. There's not a blame soul in this room who believes a single word you've been spouting.'

'I do,' Banker Pemberton said bluntly.

'And so do I,' the doctor murmured.

The mayor turned to face the medical man. 'Joe, you've known me for thirty years. How can you possibly believe all this nonsense?'

'Well, I'll tell you, Tobias. I've known Nathan for thirty years too, and his pokes missing. Now, if he killed himself, and someone let him out of the cell, someone he trusted to help him escape, then he'd go get the poke before leaving. The person who was there had to be real close kin.'

The mayor waved his hands violently. 'All right, all right. So why couldn't that fella who was kin to him have been the lad here? He's one right ambitious *hombre*. We all know that from the way he's been carryin' on. Why couldn't he have been the one?'

He looked round with an expression of triumph on his face. All that he encountered were the hard stares of men who were not convinced.

'Because he wasn't in the jailhouse,' the banker said in a loud voice.

'How the hell would you be knowin' that?'

'Because Will Vane was standing next to me as we watched it all happening from the corral behind the jailhouse.'

There was a long silence as the mayor sat down again. He seemed to collapse into the chair.

'He asked me to help him die,' he finally said. 'He was my kin and I could do no less. He didn't want to face a public hanging. It wasn't the way you're all thinking. He deserved punishment. That can't be denied, but Nathan was my kin. Surely you can understand that?'

'What about his poke?' the doctor asked mildly.

The mayor blinked. 'There was no point in leavin' money behind,' he explained. 'I'd have inherited it, anyways. If you think I done wrong, I'll resign as mayor. But I was helpin' Nathan. That's all.'

'What about the bank's money?' Will Vane asked.

'Bank money?' The mayor looked genuinely puzzled.

'When I was shot behind the bank, there were three bags of money lying on the ground. You took them away to give back to Mr Pemberton. He tells me that he only got two. One bag of notes and one of silver. Where the other one?'

'Well, with all that was going on....'

'It got mislaid,' the saloonkeeper suggested drily.

'I reckon so,' the mayor said with a feeble smile.

'Uncle Tobias,' Will Vane said softly, 'I had a long talk with Uncle Nathan last night. You silenced him too late. He told me all about the part you played in gettin' Pat Bullen away. He also mentioned a few other flim-flams you were workin' on together. Nathan knew he was goin' to hang and he didn't see no reason why he should protect you any more. He knew just as well as I did that you didn't mean to clip his ear. You meant to blow his head off.'

There was a long silence during which all eyes were focused on the mayor. He took a deep breath and got slowly to his feet again.

'There's not a lot I can say,' is there?' he said with quiet dignity. 'You've got an honest marshal runnin' the town at last and I was the one who gave him to you. They do say that no good deed goes unpunished.'